’s

ght.

matically.

ing the flat of the blade, so that it would not cut into and be trapped by the wood, he deflected the Norwegian fir shaft outwards. With the attack parried, he disengaged the sabre. Turning his hand so that the palm was uppermost, he lunged and sank the point deep into his assailant’s chest. Confronted by the onrushing bay gelding, the Lancer’s horse tried to swerve. Dusty’s mount rammed the other animal with its shoulder and knocked it staggering with a force that tore the sabre from the small Texan’s hand.

Books by J. T. Edson arranged in chronological order of stories

29. COMANCHE

Civil War Stories

THE BIG GUN*
30. THE FASTEST GUN IN TEXAS
58. KILL DUSTY FOG!
21. THE DEVIL GUN
63. UNDER THE STARS AND BARS
26. THE COLT AND THE SABRE
1. THE REBEL SPY
35. THE BLOODY BORDER
62. BACK TO THE BLOODY BORDER

The Floating Outfit Stories

4. THE YSABEL KID
56. ·44 CALIBRE MAN
64. A HORSE CALLED MOGOLLON
50. GOODNIGHT'S DREAM
51. FROM HIDE AND HORN
THE HIDE AND TALLOW MEN†
21. THE HOODED RIDERS
12. QUIET TOWN
11. TRAIL BOSS
37. WAGONS TO BACKSIGHT
48. TROUBLE RANGE
52. SIDEWINDER
20. RANGELAND HERCULES
17. MCGRAW'S INHERITANCE
38. THE HALF-BREED
44. THE WILDCATS
2. THE BAD BUNCH
54. THE FAST GUN
43. CUCHILO
9. A TOWN CALLED YELLOWDOG
41. TRIGGER FAST
46. THE TROUBLE BUSTERS
25. THE MAKING OF A LAWMAN
28. THE LAW OF THE GUN
42. THE PEACEMAKERS
66. HELL IN THE PALÒ DURO
67. GO BACK TO HELL
68. TO ARMS! TO ARMS, IN DIXIE!
69. THE SOUTH WILL RISE AGAIN
SET A-FOOT†
57. THE RUSHERS
47. THE FORTUNE HUNTERS
7. THE HARD RIDERS
14. THE RIO HONDO KID
16. WACO'S DEBT
3. THE TEXAN
34. THE FLOATING OUTFIT
55. APACHE RAMPAGE
8. RIO GUNS
60. RIO HONDO WAR
40. GUNSMOKE THUNDER
45. THE MAN FROM TEXAS
32. GUN WIZARD
36. THE SMALL TEXAN
31. THE TOWN TAMERS
53. RETURN TO BACKSIGHT
27. TERROR VALLEY
15. GUNS IN THE NIGHT

Waco Stories

24. SAGEBUSH SLEUTH
5. ARIZONA RANGER
37. WACO RIDES IN
6. THE DRIFTER
DOC LEROY M.D.†
49. HOUND DOG MAN

Calamity Jane Stories

33. COLD DECK, HOT LEAD
18. CALAMITY SPELLS TROUBLE
19. TROUBLE TRAIL
22. THE BULL WHIP BREED
10. THE COW THIEVES
61. WHITE STALLION, RED MARE
THE WHIP AND THE WAR LANCE†
13. THE BIG HUNT

John Slaughter Stories

59. SLAUGHTER'S WAY
SLAUGHTER'S NEIGHBOURS†

Waxahachie Smith Stories

NO FINGER ON THE TRIGGER†
65. SLIP GUN
WAXAHACHIE SMITH†
CURE THE TEXAS FEVER†

Rockabye County Stories

THE SHERIFF OF ROCKABYE COUNTY†
THE PROFESSIONAL KILLERS
THE ¼ SECOND DRAW
THE DEPUTIES
POINT OF CONTACT
THE OWLHOOT
RUN FOR THE BORDER
BAD HOMBRE
THEY CALL IT PROGRESS

Brady Anchor and Jefferson Trade Stories

70. TWO MILES TO THE BORDER

† In preparation

* Awaiting publication.

and published by CORGI BOOKS

J T EDSON

YOU'RE IN COMMAND NOW, MR. FOG

CORGI BOOKS
A DIVISION OF TRANSWORLD PUBLISHERS LTD
A NATIONAL GENERAL COMPANY

YOU'RE IN COMMAND NOW, MR. FOG

A CORGI BOOK 0 552 09227 4

First publication in Great Britain

PRINTING HISTORY
Corgi edition published 1973

Corgi Books are published by Transworld Publishers Ltd.,
Cavendish House, 57–59 Uxbridge Road,
Ealing, London W.5.
Made and printed in Great Britain by
Cox & Wyman Ltd., London, Reading and Fakenham

NOTE: The Australian price appearing on the back cover is the recommended retail price.

For Bob and Sue, mine host and hostess at the White Lion Hotel, Melton Mowbray; who are sufficiently strong-willed, blast them, to keep me on 'Slim-Lines' when necessary

Author's note: This book is in response to numerous readers' requests for details of Dusty Fog's early life.

Part One

THE BATTLE OF MARTIN'S MILL

CHAPTER ONE

ALTHOUGH the blue-uniformed sharpshooter sitting on a branch of the big old chestnut tree did not realize it, he was soon to cause the United States' Army of Arkansas to lose the vitally important Battle of Martin's Mill. That he brought this about would not result from incompetence. His selection of the target would be basically correct. The trouble was that he would fire too soon.

Being an ambitious professional soldier, who had adopted his specialized but frequently dangerous type of work as a means of gaining rapid promotion, the sharpshooter – in future wars the term would be changed to 'sniper' – wanted to carry out his duties in the most efficient manner possible. By doing so, he hoped to earn Colonel Middleton's approbation and maybe gain the elevation in rank that he desired.

Dispatched to carry out a routine scouting mission, he had not at first seen any hope of turning it to his advantage. In fact, he had believed that circumstances were preventing him from being with his outfit at a time when there should have been numerous opportunities to display his talents favourably to his superiors. While he had been searching the woodland, he had found himself cut off from his companions and there was clearly soon to be a battle.

From his place in the tree, he scanned – with the help of the Sharps Model of 1859 rifle's barrel-long telescopic sight

– the terrain over which the battle would be fought. Annoyance and disappointment ate at him. It seemed that he was fated to remain on the side-line. Unless something unexpected was to happen, he would be unable to do anything to further the Union's cause or to increase his hopes of obtaining promotion.

An increasing sense of frustration assailed him. In his hands he held one of the finest, most powerful, far-shooting and accurate breech-loading rifles available at that period. With it, he had been tained to the point where he could be relied upon to drive a .52 bullet into a man's chest at range of half a mile. Using a ball of soft lead, carefully shaped for its deadly purpose, such a wound was certain to incapacitate its recipient even if it did not kill him outright.

Knowing the capability of his weapon, he had chosen his point of vantage wisely on becoming aware of his predicament. The branch upon which he was seated was so massive and steady that there was no motion from it to disturb his aim. The foliage offered adequate all-round concealment, but there were sufficient gaps and openings for him to have an excellent field of vision. The full panorama of the battle-ground was spread like a map before him. All he needed was targets upon which he could practise his art.

Occupying their hastily-constructed defensive system, the remainder of the sharpshooter's regiment – the 18th 'Wisconsin' Heavy Infantry – lined their long-barrelled Springfield U.S Model of 1861 rifle-muskets. They were ready to defend the bridge across the Ouachita River against the much larger force of Confederate States' infantry and cavalry which had made its appearance and were massing for an assault.

Behind the trench lines, exposed to the sharpshooter's view by virtue of their positions, three enormous Vandenburg Volley Guns had been trained and loaded by their crews. Each Vandenburg had ninety-one separate .50 calibre barrels. When fired simultaneously, their bullets would sweep the terrain in front of the muzzle like the charge from a gigantic shotgun.

So the ugly, awkward, multi-barrelled weapons could easily prove to be a decisive factor in the forthcoming fight. They might have been damned and cursed bitterly during the march, but they were going to have a far-reaching effect on that part of the War Between The States which was being waged in Arkansas. Their presence amongst the buildings of Martin's Mill and the adjacent small hamlet did much to nullify the advantage in numbers held by the Rebels.

As on the other, better-publicized battle-fronts in the East, the Federal soldiers had the Army of the Confederate States in retreat. Being a hard-bitten realist, the sharpshooter disregarded such blindly patriotic notions as one Yankee being equal to three Johnny Rebs. Nor did he subscribe to the more religiously-inspired idea that the Good Lord was favouring the Northern cause. He accepted that superior numbers, industrial potential, technology and economics – although he would not have understood such words and would have expressed himself in more simple terms – were the chief causes of the Union's successes.

What was more, in Arkansas – no matter what rumour claimed to be happening elsewhere – the retreat was anything but a rout that had the Rebels in full flight. In fact, they were pulling back in an orderly, well-organized manner. All of their equipment and supplies were being moved towards the Ouachita River, with infantry, cavalry and artillery ably covering the withdrawal. They were effectively preventing the pursuing Union soldiers from coming even within long cannon-shot of the valuable convoy, which hardly seemed to be the actions of defeated, fleeing men.

There had recently been a change in the command of the Confederate States Army of Arkansas and North Texas. By all accounts, the new general – Ole Devil Hardin was his name – had considerable ability as a fighting man and tactician. He was playing hell with 'Cussing' Culver's often repeated boast that the Union troops would 'push those bastard-born Texas sons-of-bitches right back into their lice-infested State and make them regret the day when they first heard the word "Secession" '.

While Hardin had been unable to prevent his men from falling back, it was clear to the sharpshooter that he had them doing considerable 'pushing' on their own account. The fact was that they were just about retreating in their own good time. If they once got all their gear across the Ouachita, they would be in a fine position to prevent the Yankees from following.

Yes sir. Ole Devil Hardin was a foxy son-of-a-bitch. The way in which he had gone about shifting his supplies to safety had given proof of his shrewd tactical sense and planning ability. At first it had seemed that he intended to follow the obvious course of crossing the Ouachita near Arkadelphia. To prevent this, Culver had dispatched two cavalry regiments from his pursuing Army. After they had gone, it became obvious that Hardin had swung the column upstream.

Luckily, somebody – the sharpshooter did not credit General Culver with possessing the necessary intelligence or military knowledge – had made a shrewd guess at the supply column's destination. There was a bridge at Martin's Mill that would be capable of standing up to the heavy flow of traffic. Hardin was intending, having misled his enemies, to go over the river by the bridge. The 18th 'Wisconsin' Heavy Infantry Regiment, a half-battery of Vandenburg Volley Guns and three companies of the Long Island Lancers had been dispatched with orders to travel at their best speed and prevent the Rebels from crossing.

To the sharpshooter's way of thinking, the easiest and most effective means of carrying out their orders would have been to destroy the bridge; which could easily have been done by a smaller party. However, it seemed that General Culver had decided the bridge would be useful to his Army as they advanced to conquer Texas. So he had stated that it could only be destroyed if it was certain to fall into the enemies' hands.

Basically, Culver's plan had been good. He wanted to halt the supply column until he could bring up the full strength of his command. Then he hoped to crush the majority of military opposition in Arkansas and leave the way open for him to continue with the invasion of Northern Texas.

On either side of the trail that led to the bridge, the land rose for over a mile in a gentle, fairly even and completely open slope. Apart from the stumps of cut-down trees, it offered no shelter and could only be traversed in plain view of the defenders. There was an area of wooded land – the tree in which he sat was on the edge of it – extending at an angle from beyond the rim to join the trees and bushes which fringed the river far upstream of the bridge. It would not allow the enemy to move in close and launch an undetected flank attack. There was a similar formation on the eastern side, but even farther away from the trail, and the woods on that bank were much more open.

Any assault by the Rebels would have to be made straight down the slope, head-on to the waiting infantry, concealed Lancers and possibly unsuspected Vandenburg Volley Guns.

All in all, the situation still had much to favour the sharpshooter's party. Maybe the Rebels' advance guard had arrived way ahead of time, but they still had to make their attack across the open ground and under fire.

Suddenly it became apparent that the presence of the Vandenburgs was not unsuspected. However, their positions were causing the Rebels to attempt the counter battery work from the required direction.

Travelling at a gallop, limbered for draught, a battery of four twelve-pounder mountain howitzers* swung into sight from behind the mass of the Rebels' force. Taking advantage of the favourable nature of the terrain, they had the short-barrelled, light-weight weapons mounted on the carriages instead of being broken down into the various components and carried on the horses' pack saddles. Towed by a single

* The officially recommended number of guns in a battery was six, but that figure could rarely be made available in the Confederate States' Army.

horse, each howitzer could be moved at a swifter pace than when transported on the packs and made ready for action in a shorter time.

The Rebel artillerymen looked to be members of an efficient, well-commanded outfit. At a signal from the tall, slim, moderately handsome, dark-haired captain who led them, each chief-of-piece guided the horse which was hauling his howitzer in a tight circle. They halted with the muzzles pointing towards the village. Something over half a mile separated them from the nearest trench, which meant that they were reasonably safe from the defenders' rifle fire. However, with less than half that distance between them and the sharpshooter, they were within range of his Sharps.

In the absence of a specific target, a sharpshooter was expected to pick off the enemy's officers and deprive the enlisted men of leadership at crucial moments. There was one serious disadvantage to him taking such action. He had climbed the tree in the first place to try to ascertain the full strength of the enemy, hoping to take the news to his commanding officer. While it offered a steady base from which to do accurate shooting, he could not leave it in a hurry. Nor could he rejoin his regiment without making a lengthy detour. Each shot he fired would render his position more likely to be located and it would not be long before men were dispatched to hunt him down.

Besides which, the battery could be more effectively silenced by the Long Island Lancers. When preparing the defences, Colonel Middleton had concealed his cavalrymen in the woods fringing the upstream side of the river and had arranged the Vandenburgs accordingly. His gamble had paid off. Wanting to deal with the multi-barrelled guns as quickly as possible, the Rebel battery had taken up a position from which they could see their targets. By doing so, they had placed themselves in front of – although some distance from – where the Lancers were hidden.

Maybe the fly-slicers* were only a volunteer outfit, commanded by scent-smelling New York dudes and armed with

* Fly-slicers: derogatory name for cavalrymen.

nothing better than steel tipped wooden sticks, but there were one hundred and fifty of them against the battery's thirty-six or so. Given odds like that, the Lancers ought to be able to crush the howitzers' crews by sheer weight of numbers and far more quickly than a single rifle could do it. Nor would there be sufficient time for the Rebel cavalry on the rim to intervene, providing that the Lancers launched their attack immediately.

Sure enough, the Lancers were moving into the open.

If the sharpshooter killed the artillery captain—

Movements in the woodland, about a quarter of a mile from the chestnut tree, caught the corner of the sharpshooter's eye. Turning his head for a precautionary closer look, he was handed one hell of a shock.

Three riders were sitting their horses at the edge of the trees!

They were not alone!

Others were behind them!

Just how many more, the sharpshooter could not see. He was, however, shrewd enough to make a fairly accurate deduction.

One thing he knew for sure.

The uniforms worn by the new arrivals told him, without any question, that they were *not* members of the Federal Government's Army of Arkansas.

Studying the trio, the sharpshooter made them out to be a pair of very young lieutenants – a shavetail and a full-blown luff – and an older captain. Which implied there was at least a whole company of Confederate States' cavalry at their backs, fifty to seventy men that would be. Not just ordinary leather bumpers either, but an outfit that had already won themselves considerable acclaim as hard-fighting and very capable soldiers.

Of the three officers, the captain struck the sharpshooter as being the only one to be contended with. Tall, square-shouldered, ramrod erect on his saddle, he had a ruddy face and the hard, unsmiling features of a parade ground martinet. He looked like a German, one of the kind who called

themselves 'Prussians'. In the sharpshooter's experience, they were most unimaginative, stiff-backed, bow-necked officers with copies of the various *Manuals of Regulations* bracing their spines. Yet he knew better than to sell such men short when it came to making war, for they had been trained in such matters practically from birth. Given a military problem, they would be able to come up with an answer and it was frequently the right one.

Every inch of the captain's uniform was as stipulated in the Army of the Confederate States' *Manual of Dress Regulations.* He wore a white Jeff Davis campaign hat, with its brim down and unadorned by the plume of feathers many officers on both sides sported. In front, on the centre of the crown, was a badge formed from a silver five-pointed star in a circle. That circle would bear a laurel wreath motif and the centre of the star was embossed with the letters TLC.

Not that the sharpshooter could make out the embellishments. He was familiar with the hat badge of the Texas Light Cavalry.

Closed at the neck, the captain's stand-up collar carried the triple, three-inch long, half-inch wide strips of gold which denoted his rank. The double breasted jacket had twin rows of seven buttons. Two strands of gold braid were formed into a 'chicken guts' Austrian knot at the cuffs of the sleeves and the skirt extended correctly to half-way between the hip and the knee. Yellow-striped riding breeches ended in Hessian boots that still retained something of what must, on more suitable occasions, have been an almost mirror-like shine. The same attention had been given to his weapon belt – which the sharpshooter was willing to bet had once been fastened by a U.S. Army's buckle. It supported a sabre on the left and a revolver in a butt-forward, closed topped holster at the right. His saddle was an officer's issue McClellan, again most likely stemming from the days before he had seceded from the Union and ridden South.

Everything about the captain suggested tough, capable military efficiency. He would be fully aware of the danger to the battery and, most likely, was already formulating the means to protect the howitzers.

Neither of the junior officers appealed to the sharpshooter as being worthy of consideration on that score. From their appearances, they were a pair of rich young sprouts who had been handed their commissions because of the wealth and influence wielded by their families. In general, their uniforms followed that of the captain. Probably it was at his insistence that they stuck so closely to what was required by the *Dress Regulations.* It was unlikely that either had much military training, or control over the enlisted men.

The shavetail matched the captain in height, with wide shoulders and a build that hinted at strength. Tilted back on his head, the Jeff Davis hat exposed rumpled, untidy, curly, fiery red hair. There was something cheerfully pugnacious about his freckled, ruggedly handsome young face. It suggested that he possessed a reckless, impulsive nature. Only one bar graced a collar that would most likely have been open had he been permitted to follow his inclinations. Likewise, his 'chicken guts' were formed from a single braid.

Still only in his late teens, the second-lieutenant looked like a hot-head who would not be over-fond of discipline, nor well-versed in military strategy. He sat his big brown horse with the easy grace of a natural rider, afork a low-horned, double-girthed saddle that was definitely not an official Government issue.

Apparently the luff was somebody important's favourite son, or nephew. The sharpshooter could imagine no other reason to account for him having attained that rank. In age, he would probably match that of the shavetail – a young eighteen, at most – but he was nowhere such a fine physical specimen.

Although no more than five foot six inches in height, the luff had a sturdy enough figure. It might, the sharpshooter told himself, be more the result of a tailor's efforts than natural. Dusty blond hair showed from under his Jeff Davis hat and his tanned face was fairly good looking. However, nothing suggested to the Yankee watcher that other than family connections had pinned the second gold strip to his collar. He too used one of these hefty and – to the sharpshooter's Eastern-raised eyes – unusual saddles. Like the shavetail, he looked completely at ease on the back of the large bay gelding. Which proved little. Most rich kids, particularly down South, were taught to ride early and given ample opportunities to improve their equestrian skills.

The trio remained in cover, studying the open ground and taking notice of all that developed. At first, their attention was directed at the mountain battery and they appeared to be discussing it. While the shavetail and the captain talked, the short-grown luff continued to dart around what the watcher regarded as being nervous and anxious glances. So, not surprisingly, it was he who first observed the appearance of the Long Island Lancers and he drew his companions' attention to them.

Directing the telescopic sight at the captain's face, the sharpshooter saw that he was speaking. He appeared to be telling the first lieutenant to go somewhere, then addressed the shavetail. Most likely he would be making arrangements to lead his men to the battery's rescue. In which case, he must be stopped. A surprise attack from the flank might easily throw the Lancers into confusion. Freshly recruited back East, as yet untried in combat, armed with what the sharpshooter – and many better-informed, senior soldiers – regarded as hopelessly obsolete and antiquated weapons, they were such an uncertain element that he felt disinclined to rely upon their stability when they came under fire. Especially against the well-led, battle-hardened veterans of the Texas Light Cavalry.

Excitement filled the sharpshooter as he laid his sights on the captain's head. Here was his chance to take a significant part in the battle. By killing the captain, he would put that undersized luff in command. That would ensure the destruction of the battery, allowing the Vandenburgs to do their work without interruption.

Satisfied that he was laying the foundations of his promotion, the sharpshooter squeezed the trigger. He felt the hard thrust of the recoil against his left shoulder and the swirling gasses from the detonated powder momentarily obscured the target. Not that he doubted he had held true. His shooting instincts reassured him that he had aimed correctly. Sure enough, as the smoke was wafted away in the breeze, he saw the captain pitching from the saddle. The campaign hat had been torn off by the bullet and the captain's skull was a bloody ruin. There was no doubt that he had been killed instantly.

A crackling and crashing amongst the bushes not far from the chestnut tree caused the sharpshooter to look away from his victim. Bursting into view, glaring upwards, was a tall, lean, Indian-dark corporal of the Texas Light Cavalry. He was on foot, but moving with a deadly purpose that was menacing in the extreme. Skidding to a halt, he snapped the butt of his Henry rifle upwards, sighting straight at the sharpshooter's hiding place.

Even as the Yankee soldier tried to work the triggerguard lever as a preliminary to reloading, flames spiked wickedly from the Henry's muzzle. Slashing through the foliage, a flat-nosed ·44 calibre bullet ploughed into his left breast. Letting the rifle slip through his fingers, he followed it as it fell out of the tree. He was dead before his body struck the ground. So he never learned how he had made the mistake that would cause the Union Army to lose the Battle of Martin's Mill.

CHAPTER TWO

'HERE comes good old Doug – Captain Staunce and his boys,' announced Second Lieutenant Charles William Henry Blaze, whose ever-untidy, fiery thatch of hair had affixed to him the sobriquet 'Red', pointing to the mountain battery. 'They can sure handle those wheel-guns.'

The change in the wording of Red's first sentence had been brought about by a belated recollection of how his Company's commanding officer regarded over-familiarity between the various grades of rank. Having caught the cold glare of disapproval darted his way by the captain, he had revised his comment and made it more acceptable.

Despite the alteration, Captain Otto von Hertz continued to scowl. A young man like Mr. Blaze would never have been permitted to attain officer's status in the Prussian Army, especially in the cavalry. In von Hertz's opinion, the red head lacked the necessary aptitude to control the enlisted men, or to maintain discipline. He was far too lax and easy-going in his ways for that, despite being a member of one of the trio of Texas families whose money had recruited, equipped and organized the regiment in which von Hertz was serving.

The Prussian had to admit that the majority of the Fogs, Blazes and Hardins in the Texas Light Cavalry were capable and efficient officers, if somewhat unorthodox in many of their methods. Von Hertz's second-in-command was one of that number.

In spite of First Lieutenant Dustine Edward Marsden Fog's lack of formal military training and background, von Hertz considered him to have the makings of a very good officer and soldier. The small Texan had already proven himself capable of handling men and appeared to have gained the respect of the hardbitten veterans of Company 'C'. All in all, he was a much more satisfactory subordinate than the captain had expected at their first meeting.

'I hope they can handle them well enough,' von Hertz answered, turning his gaze to the howitzers. 'The Vandenburgs will tear the infantry to pieces unless they are silenced.'

Several years of living in the United States had failed to remove completely the harsh, Teutonic timbre from Captain von Hertz's voice. Nor could he ever obliterate the suggestion that he was consciously forcing himself to speak in what he would always regard as a foreign language. In moments of stress, he had been known to revert explosively to his native German; which was mighty disconcerting to the majority of the Texans under his command. They spoke only English, with maybe some Spanish, or an Indian dialect thrown in.

All through the years in which he had served, first in the Federal then the Confederate States' Armies, von Hertz had regretted that he could not drill the men under his command to the rigidly disciplined precision attained by German soldiers. He had managed to instil some military training into the members of Company 'C' and could count on them to carry out his orders. It was not enough for his own satisfaction, but ought to be adequate whilst carrying out the duty to which they had been assigned.

While his cousin and von Hertz watched the battery dashing to a position from which it could bombard the Vandenburgs, First Lieutenant Dusty Fog was subjecting the whole area to a thorough scrutiny. In particular, he studied the woodland fringing the river. That was where the counter-measures against the howitzers could be expected to make an appearance. Soon, too, he would be going there to carry out a delicate, difficult and dangerous mission. So he wished to form an impression of what he might be headed into.

The sharpshooter would have been amazed if he had known the nature of the assignment which had been given to that small, insignificant-seeming youngster.

A quarter of a mile was not a distance over which a detailed examination of a person could be made, even with the aid of a powerful telescopic sight. So the sharpshooter had missed much that would have been informative about Dusty Fog's appearance. Nor was the soldier given to forming a deep analysis of character. He tended to allow his first impressions to rule his judgment. If he had been a more perceptive man, he might have reached a very different opinion regarding the short first lieutenant and been less likely to think of him as a 'luff', the highly derogatory term for one of his rank.

There was an air of command about Dusty Fog which would have been obvious to more discerning eyes than those of the sharpshooter. Young, but already blooded in battle, Dusty Fog was ready, willing and able to accept responsibility. Nor was his attitude born out of a cocky, arrogant, over-inflated self-importance which had been sponsored by the knowledge that he had powerful family connections and influence behind him. He had none of the bombast that often came when a small, very young man found himself in a position of authority over his physical superiors. Instead, he carried himself with the undefinable assurance of one who had been born with the gift of leadership.

If the sharpshooter had taken the trouble to look, think and deduce, instead of dismissing Dusty as a 'luff', there were many pointers to his true potential. The horse was one. Almost seventeen hands, it was a blaze-faced bay gelding which showed power, speed and spirit in its every line. Only a strong, exceptionally capable rider could handle such a mount. Dusty occupied its Texas range saddle in a relaxed effortless manner that emphasized he was in complete command. Yet his control had not been established by cruelty, or imposed by such heavy-handed dominance that the animal no longer had a will of its own.

What the watcher in the chestnut tree took to be anxiety and nervousness, as the small Texan continually scanned the surrounding terrain, was no more than natural caution mingled with an awareness of various possibilities. Dusty was searching for anything that might interfere with the plans that his uncle, General Ole Devil Hardin, had made for capturing and holding the bridge until the supply column had crossed. Wishing to avoid drawing attention to Martin's Mill, Ole Devil had not caused it to be guarded. Instead, he had been counting on taking the Yankees by surprise; but had not left that to chance.

Presented with the duty of scouting the area the previous afternoon, von Hertz had assigned the task to two of the half-a-dozen Prussian-born soldiers who had served with him in the United States' Army before accompanying him to the South at the start of the War Between The States. There were, Dusty had considered, several men better suited to carry out the duty. His opinion had not been sought and, when he had hinted at it, von Hertz had claimed that none of the Texans – experienced Indian fighters though they undoubtedly were – possessed the military training to form a correct assessment of the situation. The two men had returned with what, on the face of it, had been adequate information.

According to von Hertz's scouts, the citizens of Martin's Mill had fled and left the hamlet unoccupied when the enemy had made an appearance. A battalion of Lancers had accompanied the 18th 'Wisconsin' Heavy Infantry and the three Vandenburg Volley Guns, but had taken an almost immediate departure in the direction from which they had come. Following their orders to the letter, the scouts had returned as soon as they had seen the Yankees taking up defensive positions on the northern side of the river.

It would have been better, Dusty had believed, if the scouts had displayed more initiative and less blind obedience to orders. One of them should have continued to keep the Yankees under observation, while the other returned with the information they had already gathered. Instead, they had followed the captain's instructions to the letter and without having attempted to think for themselves.

Fortunately, von Hertz had agreed with Dusty on one

point. The departure of the Lancers did not necessarily mean that they could be discounted as a factor. Suspecting that there might be scouts watching them, they might have been playing tricky. After giving the impression that they had left, they could easily have doubled back after dark and concealed themselves ready to take cards once the fighting began.

If Dusty had been in command of Company 'C', he would have chosen men used to thinking for themselves and told them to—

'Everything is ready for you to carry out your assignment, Mr. Fog?' von Hertz inquired, diverting the small Texan's thoughts from the men he would have selected for the scouting mission and the discretionary instructions he would have given to them.

'Yes, sir,' Dusty replied.

'Corporal Cotton hasn't returned, I see,' the captain went on coldly.

'No, sir,' Dusty admitted and glanced to where a short, white-haired, old corporal and six private soldiers sat their horses some feet away from the remainder of the Company. 'I've told Corporal Hassle to come with me if Kiowa's not back in time.'

'You should have consulted with me before sending Cotton to scout the woods!' von Hertz protested indignantly. 'I'm most displeased that you did not.'

'Yes, sir,' Dusty said, in a flat, expressionless tone.

'There was no need to send him,' von Hertz went on. 'Even if the Yankees had sent men up here to keep watch, they would already have returned to say that our force was coming.'

From the rim of the slope came the ringing notes of bugles and the rapid rolling thunder of drums. Formed up in their companies, enlisted men's bayonets and officers' swords twinkling brightly in the mid-morning sun, the 1st 'Arkansas' Rifle Regiment were commencing the assault. They intended to advance in three waves, each comprised of two companies, at two hundred yards intervals. On the flanks of the leading wave, which would bear the brunt of the attack, rode the supporting companies supplied by the Texas Light Cavalry.

At the sight and sounds of activity from the main body, von Hertz's words came to an abrupt halt. Although the captain and Red Blaze turned their eyes to the rim, Dusty continued to keep the wooded land along the northern bank of the river under observation.

'It's sure lucky those folks ran out of Martin's Mill before the Yankees arrived.' Red remarked. 'They'd've hobbled us good if some of them'd stayed in their homes.'

'We couldn't have allowed them to influence our action,' von Hertz pointed out. 'They would have had to take—'

'Just like we figured, sir,' Dusty interrupted, pointing to where the blue-clad riders were emerging. 'The Lancers did come back, all of them.'

'So they did,' von Hertz agreed, following the direction indicated by the small Texan. 'And we are ready for them. You may go and attend to your duty, Mr. Fog. Good luck.'

'Yo!' Dusty replied instantly, giving the cavalryman's traditional assent to the receipt of an order.

If the sharpshooter had refrained from firing for another minute, or even thirty seconds, Dusty Fog would have ridden away and been delayed in – maybe prevented from – taking command of the Company. The mission upon which he was about to embark had considerable urgency and was so important that he had set his horse into motion as soon as the single word had left his lips.

However, acting as he believed in the best interests of the Union, the sharpshooter selected that moment to complete his pressure on the Sharps' trigger and turned loose the bullet.

On the point of addressing Red, von Hertz took the bullet in his temple. Killed instantly, he was slammed sideways and lost his seat on the saddle. Alarmed by its rider's actions, the horse snorted and plunged forward. In death, von Hertz's left hand had tightened on the reins. So, although he was pitched lifeless to the ground, his grasp prevented the animal from running away and being seen by the enemy.

'What the—?' Red ejaculated.

Any further words were chopped off by the brown gelding moving restlessly in response to the behaviour of von Hertz's startled horse. Deftly Red regained control of his mount and swung his gaze to his cousin.

Halting his bay, Dusty twisted his torso and stared in the direction from which the shot had come. His left hand flashed across to the flap of the close-topped holster on the right of his belt. Being unable to locate the enemy sharp-shooter, he did not attempt to complete his draw. Nor, apparently, was there any need for him to do so.

'Kiowa's got the bastard!' Red guessed, when the second shot – obviously from a different weapon – sounded. 'It's lucky you sent him on that *pasear*, Cousin Dusty.'

'Not lucky enough!' Dusty growled, looking down. Hearing the startled exclamations and sounds of movement which arose from the enlisted men, he swung his attention towards them. A hard, commanding note came to his Texas drawl as he raised his voice, 'Quieten it down, damn you. Keep them back and silent, you sergeants!'

Barked-out orders from the sergeants brought about the effect desired by Dusty. While the men looked about them, searching for further enemies, they fell silent and remained in their ranks. Their concern on that score was relieved by the sound of Corporal Kiowa Cotton's voice reaching their ears.

'He's cashed and there ain't no more of them!'

Accompanied by the Company's sandy-haired. good-looking young guidon carrier and the stocky, older bugler, Sergeant Major Goering galloped forward. The bulky warrant officer sprang from his saddle and knelt at von Hertz's side. One glance told him all that he needed to know. The captain was no longer able to command Company 'C'; but there was still a vitally important duty to be carried out. So his eyes lifted towards the Company's second-in-command.

Goering had never been unduly worried about who was

placed above him in the chain of command. *Befehl ist befehl*, orders are orders, was a dictum deeply ingrained by his long years of military service. It was for the officer to make the decision on what line of action was to be taken, while Goering saw to it that his superior's wishes were carried out. However, he understood the importance of their mission and realized how high the price of failure would be.

Things could, Goering admitted to himself, be worse, Although First Lieutenant Fog lacked experience, he had the makings of a very good officer. While small, he was anything but a puny weakling. He could wield a sabre – mounted or on foot – with the best in the regiment and was the finest shot Goering had ever seen, being able to use a revolver equally well with either hand. When the occasion had demanded it, he had demonstrated bare-handed fighting techniques – learned, it was said, from General Hardin's Japanese servant – which rendered larger and stronger men helpless in his grasp.

However, the sergeant major wondered if Mr. Fog would be able to cope with the great responsibility that had been thrust upon him by Captain von Hertz's death?

Fortunately, the Company's line of action had already been decided by von Hertz when planning how to deal with the Lancers.

'The captain's dead!' Goering announced and came to his feet. Snapping into a brace as smartly as if he had been on a formal parade, he saluted and went on, 'You're in command now, Mr. Fog!'

That was one detail of which Dusty did not require to be reminded. Not only had he reached a similar conclusion, he was considering all that being left in command entailed. Yet, on the face of it, there should have been no need for him to think about how to deal with the situation.

When making arrangements to recapture the bridge, Colonel Harvey Barnett – commanding the 1st Arkansas Rifle Regiment and the assault force – had taken the danger of the Lancers' intervention into consideration. Their duty would be to nullify any attempt to bring the Vandenburgs under counter-battery fire. So he had sent Company 'C' to take up a position from which they could dash out and defend the mountain howitzers if necessary, or participate in the main attack if the need to do so did not arise.

When it had been pointed out that Company 'C' would be opposed by a force three times its size, von Hertz had declared that he was confident he could deal with the Lancers. He would offset the disparity in numbers by taking advantage of his men's superior weapons and employ a *caracole*, preventing a head-on clash that would favour the larger party. Wishing to retain as many men as possible to be thrown against the 'Wisconsins'' defences, Barnett had given his consent to von Hertz's arrangements.

Looking at the battery, Dusty discovered that Captain Douglas St. John Staunce did not intend to rely solely upon the cavalry to protect his howitzers. He had reduced each piece's crew to three men and formed up the remainder, under the command of Sergeant Major Smalley, in a fighting line between the battery and the Lancers. Even the horse-holders had been called upon to take part in the defensive duty, leaving the animals to fend for themselves.

Dusty sucked in a deep breath as he noticed the latter point. Aware of how much depended upon his howitzers being able to silence the Vandenburgs, Staunce was leaving himself without the means of retreat. Once the fighting started, the horses were certain to stampede and he would not be able to use them to haul his little guns to safety. It was clearly a case of root, hog, or die, for the men of the battery – especially if Company 'C' should fail to halt their attackers.

From examining the artillerymen and their howitzers, Dusty returned his gaze to the Lancers. They were already assembled in three waves as they emerged from concealment. Each line was formed of one company, with its officers at the front and in the centre of it. However, the waves were so close that the heads of the officers' horses were almost touching the rumps of the preceding company's mounts. Nor did they appear to be rectifying the situation.

Studying the close proximity of the Lancers' three companies, Dusty could visualize one major objection to attacking them in the manner suggested by his dead superior.

The *caracole* was one of the earliest manoeuvres to have been developed for use by cavalry carrying firearms. When charging to engage an approaching enemy, instead of meeting them head-on, the party performing the *caracole* would divide itself into two groups. Turning outwards, each section would gallop around their opponent's flanks and attack from the rear.

Under certain circumstances, a *caracole* could be a devastatingly effective tactic. It was especially useful when performed against men armed with swords or lances.*

'Shall I tell the men to move out, Mr. Fog?' Goering prompted.

'Yes,' Dusty confirmed. 'Column of twos.'

'It might be as well if I warned them we'll be doing a *caracole*, sir,' the sergeant major remarked, in polite, deferential tones.

'Don't tell them that!' Dusty snapped.

'It would be better for them to know what we're going to do,' Goering insisted, without waiting for the small Texan to continue with an explanation.

'I'm not gainsaying it, sergeant major,' Dusty replied. 'But we're not using a *caracole*.'

'Captain von Hertz said that was how—!' Goering reminded.

'The captain's dead,' Dusty interrupted. 'And, like you said, *I'm* in command now. Is that understood, sergeant major?'

'Yo!' affirmed Goering, stiffening even more into his rigid parade-ground brace. Holding his voice flatly emotionless, he went on, 'May I ask the lieutenant's intentions, sir?'

'We'll form into echelon as we leave the trees, Dusty explained, watching the sergeant major's face. 'Then we'll

* How effective a caracole could be is described in *Sidewinder*.

ride forward until we're between the battery and the Lancers. When we're there, I'll give the order to turn right and we'll charge straight at them.

Before swinging his gaze towards the mass of the Lancers, Goering's features showed a mixture of surprise and alarm. Red Blaze displayed no such misgivings. Instead, he let out a low whoop of approval.

'Yeeah! That's what I wanted to hear, Cousin Dusty!'

Neither Dusty nor Goering gave any indication that they had heard the redhead's words. Instead, their eyes met and seemed to be locked in a struggle for domination. After a couple of seconds, Goering lowered his gaze.

'They have us outnumbered, sir,' the sergeant major warned.

'I know that,' Dusty conceded. 'But my way is the only one that will stop them reaching the howitzers. There's no time to argue, or to hold a debate, sergeant major. Carry out my orders.'

For a moment Goering seemed to be on the verge of continuing his protests. Instead, his eyes flickered to the Lancers and back in Dusty's direction. Years of living under military discipline had their effect, backed by an instinctive feeling that the young officer was acting as he believed for the best. Certainly time was not available for a discussion on the matter.

'Yo!' Goering said, saluting and turning to mount his horse.

'You'll take over my detail, Cousin Red,' Dusty ordered, as Goering rode towards the enlisted men.

'Me!' Red yelped, realizing that to obey would cause him to miss out on what he figured would be a real good fight.

'You,' Dusty agreed. 'It has to be done and, way things've turned out, I can't do it. So you'll have to take my place.'

'I don't have a knife with me,' Red remarked hopefully.

'Take mine,' Dusty offered, drawing the Russell-Barlow clasp-knife from his breeches' pocket and holding it out. 'Company "A's" detail aren't likely to get through, the woods're too open on that side of the bridge. Happen you handle it the way I told you I aimed to, you'll likely get by.'

'I'll give her a whirl anyways,' Red promised, sounding resigned, and pocketed the knife. 'You figure you're playing it right, going for them head-on?'

'I figure I'm right,' Dusty declared. 'If I am, you've got to stop them blowing up the bridge.'

'Count on me to try,' Red grinned, deciding that his new assignment had possibilities of action and danger that would in some measure compensate for him missing the forthcoming battle with the Lancers. 'Good luck, Cousin Dusty.'

'And to you,' Dusty replied.

'Likely we'll both need it,' Red drawled. 'See you on the bridge.'

Watching Red join the corporal and six men of the special detail, Dusty could hear Goering passing on his orders to the remainder of the Company. So the small Texan turned his gaze once more to the open land. Everything he could see reaffirmed his belief that he had made the right decision. There was, he knew, one major objection to using the *caracole* in the prevailing conditions. So he had selected what he felt sure was the only way for his outnumbered force to give the mountain battery adequate protection.

There were also, Dusty realized, desperate risks involved.

He would be leading his men into a conflict with odds of at least three to one against them. What was more, he was disregarding the method by which his older, more experienced – now dead – superior officer had planned to deal with the situation. If Dusty was wrong and failed, the future of the Confederate States Army of Arkansas and North Texas would be placed in jeopardy.

Everything depended upon how much faith the men of Company 'C' had in their new commanding officer.

If they trusted his judgment, they would follow him.

Ever since Dusty had joined Company 'C', he had worked to earn the respect and confidence of its members. The next few minutes would show whether or not he had succeeded. Dusty thought of some of the events which, he hoped, would have helped him to gain the approbation of the men fate had placed under his command.

Part Two

THE MAKING OF A LEADER

CHAPTER THREE

DESPITE Sergeant Billy Jack's gloomy predictions on being given the assignment, he had reached Arkadelphia – seat of Clark County, Arkansas – without having been waylaid, captured, or killed by marauding Yankees. His horse had failed to throw and roll on him, there had been no lightning to strike him, nor had any of the numerous other disasters occurred that he had envisaged when discussing his mission before leaving the headquarters of the Texas Light Cavalry. Of course, he told himself with doleful satisfaction, he still had to locate the two replacement officers and twenty-four volunteers whom he had been sent to find and deliver to the regiment.

Slouching on the saddle of his powerful dun gelding, Billy Jack looked like a dejected and ill-used stork. A kepi, bearing the silver star-in-a-circle badge of the Texas Light Cavalry, perched at what – in almost any other person – would have been a jaunty angle on the back of his head. A prominent Adam's apple combined with a receding chin and thin face to give him almost miserable, careworn aspect. Tall, lanky, his rawboned, angular frame did little to set off a uniform that showed signs of the journey which he was making. He had on a waist-long tunic, yet the three chevrons on the sleeves seemed almost out of place, taken with his general appearance. About his waist hung a Western-style gunbelt, with 1860 Army Colts in the tied-down, open topped holsters. Yellow-striped riding breeches and Hessian boots served to emphasize the thinness of his legs. All in all, he did not appear to be the kind of man to hold rank of sergeant in a tough, fighting cavalry regiment.

With his horse ambling leisurely along the main street, Billy Jack wondered what kind of officers Lieutenants Fog and Blaze would develop into. He had a strong personal interest in the matter. Recently graduated from Judge Blaze's small military academy – down at Polveroso City, Rio Hondo County, Texas – they were coming to his Company and one of them was sure to become his immediate superior. So he hoped that they would prove to be satisfactory. On the face of it, there had originally seemed a better than fair chance that they might.

If the former youngster was anything like his father, Major Hondo Fog, he ought to turn into a damned good fighting cavalry leader and should be an asset to Company 'C'. Mr. Blaze already had two older brothers in the Texas Light Cavalry and they were rapidly carving names for themselves as courageous, capable and efficient officers. Billy Jack hoped that the latest arrival from the Blaze family would come up to his brothers' standards.

Trouble was that they might not come up to the high standards set by their kinsmen. Events certainly appeared to be pointing in that direction. They had been expected to arrive in Little Rock, with the twenty-four volunteers they were escorting, a week back. Needing the men, and wanting to train them before sending them into action, Colonel Blaze had dispatched Billy Jack with orders to locate them. Taking the route over which they were supposed to be travelling, Billy Jack had arrived at Arkadelphia without finding any trace of them.

Most of the evidence pointed to the two young officers having lost their way. Which did not say much for their abilities. All they had had to do was follow the route taken by Colonel Jubal Early's herders when delivering herds of cattle to help feed the Army of Arkansas and North Texas. That would have brought them to Arkadelphia and, once they had crossed the Ouachita River, there was a well-defined trail to Little Rock.

If Mr. Fog and Mr. Blaze could not follow such an obvious line of march, they would be of little use to Company 'C'.

Thinking sombrely about the two young officers. Billy Jack found himself approaching the Clinton Hotel. There were, he noticed, eight horses standing hitched to the rail outside the building. Six carried McClellan saddles and had Enfield single-shot carbines in their boots. The other pair, a big, blaze-faced bay and an equally large brown gelding were much finer animals. Each bore a good quality Texas range rig, like the one on Billy Jack's dun, with a bed roll lashed to the cantle. More significantly, each of them had a coiled rope and a sabre dangling on either side of its saddle's low horn.

In passing, then turning alongside the two horses, Billy Jack observed that there was a Henry rifle in the bay's saddleboot and the brown carried a Spencer carbine. He found the weapons less interesting than the animals' brands. The bay was marked with the letters 'O' and 'D', placed so close together that their edges touched. On the rump of the brown had been burned a pair of 'B's'.

'OD Connected and Double B,' the sergeant translated, swinging to the ground and securing the dun's reins to the hitching rail. 'Must be them, but where're the enlisted men at? Likely they've all deserted 'n' I'll get blamed for it.

With that mournful sentiment concluded, Billy Jack crossed the sidewalk. Passing through the hotels open front doors, he found its lobby deserted. He was strolling towards the reception desk, meaning to see if he could obtain information about the owners of the two horses, when he heard voices from the barroom.

'I've come to fetch you bunch out to the herd,' a young-sounding, well-educated Texas drawl was declaring. 'And I'm not about to go back without you.'

'That's the way of it, huh?' demanded a set of harsh,

rasping tones which Billy Jack believed he recognized. 'Well, Eli, Trug, Japhet, Lou 'n' Toby here's all of a mind with me, sonny. We don't take kind to no frying-size civilian delivering such messages from officer-boys.'

'We don't even take no notice when he sends *corporals* to fetch us,' stated a second familiar voice. 'But we'll not hold you coming again' you, happen you shows you're sorry by setting up the drinks.'

'That's what's knowed as an old Army custom, half-portion,' continued a third speaker, making the sergeant even more certain he knew some of the men in the barroom. 'In times of war, all civilians has to buy us fighting soldiers drinks when we asks for 'em.'

'Are *you* bunch *fighting* soldiers?' inquired the Texas drawl, every word suggesting that such a thing was highly unlikely.

'Just what do *you* reckon we are?' demanded the first of the familiar voices, throbbing with menace.

Having an idea of what might be happening, or likely to happen in the near future, Billy Jack approached the barroom. Its door was wide open and allowed him an excellent all-round view of the interior. What he saw confirmed that he did know some of the occupants and was correct in his assumptions of what they were planning to do.

Watched by the fat, bald-headed, grinning, elderly bartender, half a dozen soldiers were moving to form a loose circle around a civilian. Clad in kepis, with tunics that were unbuttoned to display dirty undershirts, riding breeches and boots, the soldiers were long-haired, unshaven and dishevelled. The bands around their hats, the stand-up collars and cuffs of their tunics and the stripes on the legs of their breeches were buff in colour. Although all wore weapon belts, only the burly corporal, who was standing directly in front of the civilian, had a holstered revolver.

Recognizing Corporal 'Bully' Chatswen and the five enlisted men, Billy Jack could see that they were going to indulge in a favourite pastime. It was called 'jostling'. Gathering around a potential victim, they would taunt and harass him in the hope that he would be goaded into attacking one of them. Once that happened, the rest would watch and enjoy the fight – or help if it seemed likely that their companion was getting beaten.

There had been an occasion, in this same barroom, when Chatswen and is companions had selected Billy Jack for their victim. He doubted whether they would have forgotten how their 'jostling' had been turned into a painful disaster, due to his unexpected ability to defend himself and the fortuitous arrival of four more members of Company 'C'.

Possibly Chatswen's party had profited from that unfortunate and painful experience. While they had apparently not given up 'jostling', they had at least grown more discriminating in their selection of a victim. From all appearances, their current potential recipient hardly seemed capable of producing any serious or dangerous resistance.

Standing with his back to Billy Jack, confronted and almost dwarfed by the bulky, black-haired Corporal Chatswen, the civilian was no more than five foot six inches in height. He had no hat and his hair was a dusty blond colour. The scarlet silk bandana, tight rolled and knotted about his throat, black and white calfskin vest, grey shirt, brown trousers, with their cuffs turned back and hanging outside high heeled boots, were the working clothes of a Texas cowhand.

Although Billy Jack could not see the small Texan's face, his general appearance and the references made to his youth by the soldiers suggested that he was much younger as well as smaller and lighter than his tormentors. Yet, despite the fact that he did not appear to be armed in any way, he displayed little concern over their threatening attitudes or the fact that they were surrounding him. Probably, the sergeant concluded, the cowhand did not appreciate his peril. Certainly his response to Chatswen's challenging question was not that of a frightened young man.

'From what I've seen of you,' the Texan drawled, in tones as gentle as the first menacing whispers of a blue norther storm blowing up. 'You're what I've heard are called "too-fars".'

At that moment, Billy Jack noticed the second of the room's doors was slowly easing open. He could not see who, or what, might be at the other side and the continuation of the conversation diverted his attention back to the speakers.

'"Too-fars"?' repeated Chatswen, looking puzzled. 'Just what the hell're "too-fars"?'

'Fellers who're too far forward to wash and shave,' answered the small Texan, apparently oblivious of Trug moving to stand behind him. 'But too far away from the fighting to get shot at.'

Billy Jack decided that although the blond had shown a shrewd judgment of the soldiers' characters, he could not be considered a person of tact, diplomacy, or even of good sense. There was little else that the youngster could have said which would have been more likely to bring Chatswen's wrath down upon him. Serving in the Commissary General's Department, the corporal and his five companions had never seen active duty. They were employed to collect and complete the delivery of the cattle which Colonel Jubal Early's trail crews had driven from Texas. Their work was of considerable importance to the Confederate States' war effort, but that did not alter the fact of them never having engaged in combat with the enemy. So they strenuously resented any comments on the matter; especially when such were made by a small, insignificant-looking civilian.

'And you figure's me 'n' the boys're these-here "too-fars"?' Chatswen challenged, while his companions rumbled menacingly.

'That's what I figure,' confirmed the Texan, apparently glancing to where Eli had moved forward from between Japhet and Lou. Or he could, Billy Jack realized, have been looking at the partially open side door beyond the three soldiers. 'And nothing I've seen of you yet's come close to making me think I *might* not be right about it.'

'You hear that, Hervey?' Chatswen said to the bartender. 'This short-grown runt's disrespecting us.'

'That's what he's doing, Billy,' agreed the fat, bald

civilian. 'Nobody'd blame you should you get riled about it.'

'So that's the way it goes, huh?' drawled the small Texan, without looking at the bartender. 'I figured it would be something like that. All right, I'm through asking. Let's have you out of here and on your horses—'

'Boy!' Chatswen interrupted, advancing and reaching with a ham-like right hand towards the diminutive – in comparison with his own bulk – young figure. 'I'm going to teach you some respect—'

Billy Jack found himself on the horns of a dilemma over what, if any, action he should take. Being in Arkadelphia on official business, he had no desire to become involved in a barroom brawl. Especially when the bartender invariably backed up the excuses of his good customers. Yet the sergeant could hardly stand by and watch a fellow-Texan – no matter how undiplomatic or rash – being assaulted by the larger, heavier soldiers.

To intervene, however, would invite painful repercussions. There was little love lost between the men of the Texas Light Cavalry and Chatswen's bunch. Secure in the knowledge that Hervey would support their stories in the event of an inquiry, the six men would resist any orders that Billy Jack might attempt to give to them. Instead, they would turn part of their wrath on him. That meant he would have to take them on with only such small help as the young blond could muster. There was no other assistance available.

Confident in the advantages granted by his extra size and weight, Chatswen saw no call for caution. Probably, on realizing that he had bitten off a whole heap more than he could chew, the runty beef-head* would attempt to jump backwards or try to run away. In either event, Trug was positioned so as to cut off his retreat.

Deciding to use his Colts as a means of enforcing his demands, Billy Jack dropped his hands to the butts as he stepped into the barroom. The other door was thrown open, but the sergeant's attention was held by Chatswen and the blond.

* Beef-head: derogatory name for a Texan.

Instead of retreating in an attempt to avoid being caught by the corporal's reaching fist, the small Texan moved swiftly to meet him. Chatswen's brain failed to react swiftly enough to assess and counter such an unexpected development. Up flashed the blond's left hand. The corporal felt his right wrist grasped with surprising strength and it was jerked forward. Nor did that end his misfortunes. Spreading his feet apart and bowing his knees, the Texan darted his right hand between Chatswen's thighs and took hold of the slack seat of his breeches.

Just what was happening, neither Billy Jack, Chatswen or the other soldiers could have said. Continuing to move with such speed that the corporal had no opportunity to resist, the small Texan ducked his head under the captured arm and tilted Chatswen's bulky torso across his shoulders. With a surging heave that told of considerable muscular power behind it, the blond straightened his legs. Elevating the amazed corporal from the floor, he pivoted and, lowering his head, pitched Chatswen into the advancing Trug's arms. Letting out mutually startled yells, the two men toppled to the floor in a tangled heap.

Like Billy Jack, who had halted with his Colts still in leather and mouth open but not emitting any words, the remaining soldiers were frozen into immobility by what they had seen. Possibly only the sergeant was aware of another element about to enter the game.

Tall, well-built, about the same age as the small blond, a second cowhand entered. He came through the side door, grinning delightedly as he darted swiftly across the room. Bare-headed and unarmed, he had untidy, fiery red hair and a freckled, pugnaciously handsome face.

Amazed by what he had seen happen to Chatswen, the bartender failed to give a warning of the newcomer's presence. Not that his omission left the soldiers in complete ignorance of the danger. The red-head made his presence felt swiftly enough.

Coming from behind the unsuspecting Japhet and Lou, the red-head bounded into the gap between them. He threw open his arms, enfolding their necks from the rear and clamping home in a determined, forceful manner.

'Dusty!' whooped the newcomer, swinging up his feet and bringing his full weight to bear on the two soldiers.

Thrusting forward, the red-head's high-heeled boots thudded into the centre of Eli's back and he was sent hurtling in the small Texan's direction. Flailing wildly with his arms, Eli bore down rapidly upon the blond. The soldier was big and brawny enough to have come off best in the event of a collision, but such a fortunate result was denied to him.

In turning to throw Chatswen at Trug, the small Texan had allowed Billy Jack to see his face. Tanned, grey-eyed, not too bad looking, the features put the sergeant in mind of somebody and supplied a clue to the blond's identity. That wrestling throw, too, was much like one Billy Jack had seen performed by Ole Devil Hardin's servant, a smallish, smiling man who claimed to hail from some place called 'Nippon'. That too was suggestive of who the young cowhand might be.

All of which was driven from the sergeant's thoughts as he watched Eli hurtling on a collision course for the short youngster. Even as the sergeant prepared to deliver a warning, he saw that the blond had heard and understood the red-head's shouted work.

Turning fast, the blond stepped to the left sufficiently far to avoid being struck by the rushing soldier. Nor did he restrict his attentions to mere evasion. Knotting his right hand, he threw a punch. Watching the hand sink almost wrist-deep into Eli's ample belly, Billy Jack could nearly sympathize with his agony-filled gurgling croak as he folded over. Blundering onwards, clutching at his mid-section as he moaned and gasped for breath, Eli reached the bar and collapsed, retching, by it.

Taken by surprise by the red-head's unexpected intervention, Japhet and Lou had not been able to resist. His weight caused them to bend forward and he retained his hold on their necks. Bracing himself on spread-apart feet and leaning backwards, he exerted his strength to prevent them from straightening up and getting free.

'Now this pair, Cousin Dusty!' the red-haired youngster called.

Almost as if working to a preconceived plan, the blond ignored the stricken Eli and darted towards the entangled trio. Bounding from the floor, he propelled his feet against the tops of Lou's and Japhet's heads. At the moment of impact, displaying superb timing, the red-head released his hold and the assaulted pair went reeling backwards. They landed on their rumps at practically the same moment, then flopped supine with dazed, glassy-eyed expressions on their unprepossessing faces.

'I thought I said for you to throw down on them with your Colts—' the blond said as he alighted from the bounding kick which had once more reminded Billy Jack of a trick used by Tommy Okasi.

Looking like a man waking from a nightmare, Toby stared from one to another of his companions. Although Chatswen and Trug had rolled apart, neither had yet succeeded in rising. From all appearances, the remainder of the party were no longer actively interested in the affair. That, Toby decided, put matters in his hands. Figuring to uphold his bunch's reputation for toughness – and to take the cowhands by surprise – he lumbered rapidly in their direction. Being a slugger, who relied on brawn instead of skill, he was basing his attack's success on a bull-like rush. It should, he concluded, be easy. Having felled Lou and Japhet in that sneaky, tricky way, the cowhands were talking to each other and not watching him.

'Shucks, don't be a spoilsport, Cous—' the red-head protested, then glanced towards Toby. 'Look out!'

Once again the youngsters displayed a teamwork which Billy Jack watched with admiration. Spinning swiftly, the blond stepped aside to avoid being struck by the heavier man. Advancing, the red-head moved in the opposite direction when level with his cousin. Unable to halt in time, Toby started to pass between them and his big hands grasped empty air. Out flashed two fists, their knuckles connecting on each side of Toby's jaw. The soldier's eyes glazed and, carried forward by his impetus, he kept moving until his knees buckled and deposited him face down on the floor.

Paying no greater attention to Toby than he had to his other victims, the small blond swung to face Chatswen as the corporal lurched erect.

'I sent my corporals into town last night with a message for you,' the Texan said quietly, shaking and working the fingers of the hand that had struck Toby's jaw. 'You got them into a fight, beat them up and sent word that I should come myself. So I'm here.'

'You bastard!' Chatswen bellowed, so furious that he failed to understand the full implications of what he was hearing. Instead, he hurled himself bodily at the small blond. 'I'll fix your wag—!'

Having allowed his Colts to settle back in their holsters, on being satisfied that the young Texans did not require that kind of assistance. Billy Jack had remained in the doorway. Leaning his shoulder against the jamb. he watched Chatswen bearing down massively upon the shorter cowhand.

Exactly what happened after that the sergeant could not be certain. Once again the blond caught the corporal by an arm, pivoted and Chatswen sailed almost gracefully over his shoulder. Landing on a table, Chatswen's weight collapsed it and he was dumped on to the floor. Muttering profane threats, he rose and rushed at his tormentor.

While Billy Jack had no liking for Chatswen, he felt nearly sorry as he watched the corporal receive one hell of a thrashing. Not only did the small Texan know a number of wrestling throws and holds which more than off-set his lack of size, he was remarkably strong and could use his fists with devastating effectiveness. When Chatswen received a final series of crashing punches that tumbled him limply into a corner, he had been as thoroughly beaten as had any of his 'jostling' victims.

Leaving his cousin to deal with the corporal, the red-head had taken on Trug. To Billy Jack, it seemed that the taller cowhand was delighted with the opportunity of a fight. They were evenly matched in size and weight, but the Texan was younger, fitter and more skilful. So, although he took some punishment himself and was far less spectacular in his methods, he handed out nearly as painful a battering.

'What happened to my corporals last night?' the blond demanded, crossing to the bar after glancing in Billy Jack's direction.

'They come in and started getting all uppy with Bully and the boys—' the bartender began, trying to repay the soldiers for the business they had put his way.

'*They* started it, huh?' the blond grunted.

'You might say that,' Hervey agreed, feeling uneasy as cold grey eyes seemed to be boring into his inner thoughts.

'It's not likely I would, being raised to speak the truth,' interrupted the blond.

'Are you saying I'm lying,' Hervey demanded, sounding a whole heap tougher and indignant than he felt.

'Let's put it you're just being loyal to good customers,' drawled the blond. 'You all right, Cousin Red?'

'*Bueno*, Cousin Dusty,' grinned the red head, dabbing at his bloody nose with a bandana. 'I'll go fetch our hats and gunbelts.'

'You do that,' the blond confirmed and turned his attention back to the bartender. 'Get those yahoos on their feet. Tell them to meet me down at the livery barn in half an hour. If they're longer than that, I'll come back and fetch them – and, mister, if that happens, I'll not be coming peaceable.'

'Bully and the boys won't like me telling them that,' Hervey objected, wondering how one so young and small could make him feel uneasy.

'Tell them I'll be waiting at the barn and they can take it up with me there,' ordered the blond and swung to face Billy Jack. 'Howdy, sergeant. I reckon you might be looking for me.'

'Likely, sir,' Billy Jack admitted, snapping into a brace and saluting. 'Unless I'm wrong, which I admit I most times am, you'll be Lieutenant Fog.'

CHAPTER FOUR

'THEY'RE coming, Mr. Fog,' Sergeant Billy Jack announced dolefully, while his lean features registered what seemed to be considerable alarm and despondency. 'Only I don't reckon it's 'cause they've figured out who you are and're all respectful of your rank.'

'Maybe not,' Dusty Fog drawled, also glancing overtly to where Corporal Chatswen's detail were approching. They were leading their horses and the enlisted men held the Enfield carbines which had previously been in the saddle-boots, while the flap of the corporal's holster was open and tucked back. 'Don't let on we've seen them.'

'Yo!' Billy Jack assented and swung his gaze to where Red Blaze was standing the last of half a dozen empty whisky bottles on the top rail of an unused corral. 'We could allus mount up and ride to the herd for help.'

'I'd sooner stop here and see what they're planning to do,' Dusty replied, having realized just how little of the sergeant's attitude and general line of speech was genuine. 'You never know, we might all get ourselves killed and save the Yankees the trouble of doing it.'

'I ain't likely to be *that* lucky,' Billy Jack protested dismally. 'It'll only be you'n' Mr. Blaze's dies and I'll have to go back 'n' tell Captain von Hertz I couldn't carry out his orders.'

'Well now,' Dusty grinned. 'I sure wouldn't want *you* to have to do that. So we'll see if we can sort of dissuade these "too-fars" from abusing us.'

'I surely hope we can,' Billy Jack admitted, in tones which implied that he felt it was highly unlikely. 'Now if them bottles was full—'

'It'd be a sinful shame and wasteful of good whisky,' Dusty finished.

'Never knowed Hervey selled any *good* whisky,' Billy Jack objected, wondering just what the small young officer had had in mind when asking him to obtain the six empty bottles before they had left the hotel.

Having donned the gunbelt and hat which Red had collected from the hall outside the barroom's side door, Dusty had accompanied his cousin and the sergeant to the rendezvous he had designated to the bartender.

The livery barn was situated on the edge of town. Leaving the horses – Billy Jack had been correct in his assumption of who owned them – outside the main building, Dusty had led the way to the empty corral. There he had requested that Red should stand the bottles on the side of the fence farthest away from the town. Grinning at the mystified expression on the sergeant's face, the red-head had complied. Ignoring Billy Jack's obvious puzzlement, Dusty had continued with his explanation of what had led up to the confrontation at the Clinton Hotel.

Given the acting rank of first lieutenant, Dusty had been put in command of a party of recruits on their way to join the Texas Light Cavalry. As they had ridden north, they had come across Colonel Jubal Early of the Commissary General's Department. The colonel had just purchased a herd of cattle for delivery to the Army of Arkansas and North Texas, but had wished to take up an offer of an even larger bunch made by a rancher in Denton County. Knowing that most of the recruits had been cowhands, Dusty had offered to drive the herd to Arkadelphia. Doing so would delay the party's arrival at Little Rock, but he had believed that he was acting for the best. Early had accepted, with the proviso that one of his experienced sergeants should accompany the cattle. An accident while crossing the Red River had deprived Dusty of the sergeant's services, but he had been successful in handling the trail drive without the expert's advice.

Reaching the Arkadelphia area the previous night, Dusty had bedded the herd down a couple of miles from the town. The cattle had been restless, so he and Red had remained with them. Knowing that a party from the Commissary General's Department were to take charge of the cattle at that point, Dusty had sent the two youngsters he had appointed acting corporals to carry word of their arrival. The corporals had located Chatswen's detail, who were drinking at the Clinton Hotel. On hearing Dusty's message, Chatswen had 'jostled' the corporals and provoked a fight. He had then sent back the beaten Texans with a message to the effect that Lieutenant Fog should come in and tell Chatswen himself and not send wet-behind-the-ears underlings.

'I reckon he figured that he was dealing with a couple of fuzz-faced, inexperienced shavetails and could get away with it,' Dusty had commented. 'Or he allowed to say he'd never said any such thing and could count on that fat bartender to back up any lies he told.'

'Hervey'd do that for sure,' Billy Jack had conceded.

Realizing that he could not overlook such a flagrant disrespect of his authority, Dusty had been determined to take action. When Chatswen's detail had not reached the herd by about ten o'clock in the morning, he had gone to find them accompanied by Red.

'I reckoned that those yahoos wouldn't show too much respect for a young lieutenant, especially one who wasn't in their outfit,' Dusty had explained. 'So I knew that I'd get no place walking in and flashing my collar bars. That's why I'm wearing my civilians clothes.'

At the hotel, following the plan formulated by Dusty during the ride to town, Red had taken Dusty's gunbelt and hat, while Dusty had entered the barroom Red had taken up his position outside the second door. The red-head was supposed to make his appearance and, using his Colts to enforce his demand, compel the enlisted men to stand aside while Dusty had dealt with Chatswen. That had not appealed to Red's ebullient nature and, seeing how the men had positioned themselves around Dusty, he had taken the opportunity to shed his own weapons and take a more active part in the scheme.

During the walk from the hotel, Billy Jack had warned Dusty that the soldiers were unlikely to forget, or forgive, the humiliation and punishment they had received. They were, the sergeant had continued, likely to come looking for evens. In which case, having failed with their fists, they might conclude to call the next play with guns. Much to Billy Jack's surprise, Dusty had appeared to be inclined to overlook the possibility. Red Blaze had declared cheerfully that everything was liable to work out fine.

Having noticed the menacing attitudes and held weapons of the approaching men, Billy Jack felt that he had guessed correctly about how they planned to take their revenge. However, he also had a suspicion that Mr. Fog was not only aware of the danger, but had something in mind to circumvent it.

'All set, Cousin Dusty,' Red announced cheerily. 'Don't them blasted "too-fars" look all mean 'n' ornery, though?'

'That they do,' Dusty admitted, showing just as little sign of knowing that Chatswen's detail were drawing nearer and fanning into a line. 'Reckon this's going to work, Cousin Red?'

'Happen it don't, I'll never speak to you again,' Red grinned. 'What do you think, Billy Jack?'

'That I don't know what to think,' the sergeant groaned, looking worried and not a little afraid. 'I'll be pleased when it's all over. Happen I live through it, that is.'

'Don't you get killed before I've finished,' Dusty said. 'That's an order.'

With that, the small Texan started to walk across the corral towards the bottle-decorated fence. Billy Jack's panic-stricken aspect departed and he divided his attention between watching Dusty and covertly keeping the soldiers under observation. He noticed that Chatswen's party were also watching the young blond and appeared puzzled by what they were seeing.

Halting when he was about twenty-one feet from the fence, Dusty stood on spread-apart, slightly bent legs. At the same instant, his hands flashed inwards. Crossing, they swept the bone-handled Colts from the carefully-designed holsters. Thumbing back the hammers and slipping his forefingers into the triggerguards only *after* the barrels had cleared leather, Dusty aimed from waist level and by instinctive alignment. Just three-quarters of a second after his hands' first movements, flame licked out of the muzzles of the Colts and their detonations came almost as a single sound.

With the exception of Red, who was aware of his cousin's ambidextrous ability, the watching men believed that Dusty had only fired once. Startled exclamations rose from Chatswen's detail when the bottles at each end of the line disintegrated simultaneously. Even Billy Jack, who was no slouch when it came to handling a brace of Army Colts, was impressed by the small Texan's lightning speed and double-handed accuracy. Nor did the display end there.

Cocking each Colt as its seven-and-a-half inch 'Civilian Model' barrel* reached the height of its recoil, Dusty turned the muzzles inwards. Without raising the revolvers higher or taking more careful sight, he continued to throw lead. As the Colts roared, the bottles shattered and he never missed. On destroying the final pair, he twirled the weapons on his trigger-fingers and returned them to their holsters almost as swiftly as they had emerged.

Turning, Dusty strolled to where Red and Billy Jack were standing side by side. If the lanky sergeant's face was showing admiration, it was nothing to the expressions being exhibited by the other soldiers. All had come to a halt and were staring in alarmed, awe-filled amazement.

As if becoming aware for the first time of Chatswen's detail being around, Dusty swung towards them. His eyes went to the carbines, dropped briefly at the opened flap of the corporal's holster, then lifted and raked the men's faces.

* Colt 1860 Army revolvers intended for sale to the military had eight inch barrels.

Not one of them would meet the cold scrutiny. Even Chatswen lowered his head to hide his confusion and uncertainty.

'Are you expecting trouble from the Yankees, corporal?' Dusty demanded, walking closer to the soldiers.

'Huh?' Chatswen ejaculated, jerking up his face and staring in a puzzled manner at the small Texan.

Except that Dusty no longer seemed small, or insignificant. In some mysterious manner, he appeared to have grown until he bettered the corporal in size.

'I said are you expecting trouble with the Yankees?' Dusty repeated.

'What Yankees?' Chatswen wanted to know.

'If there aren't any, why the hell are your men carrying their carbines?' Dusty snapped. 'And why isn't your holster flap fastened down?'

'I—' Chatswen began.

'Are there any Yankees hereabout, sergeant?' Dusty asked over his shoulder, without taking his gaze from the soldiers.

'Nary a one's I knows about, *Lieutenant* Fog, sir,' Billy Jack answered, guessing correctly how Dusty wanted the reply to be worded.

'I reckon we can take your word on that,' Dusty drawled and stared hard at Chatswen. 'Don't you, corporal?'

For a moment the burly non-com did not reply. Clearly Hervey had been telling the truth, when he had claimed that the short-grown – or *very big* – blond son-of-a-bitch was an officer. Which put an entirely different complexion on the matter, despite Chatswen's assertions that not even a blasted officer could treat him in such a fashion and live to boast about it.

'Yeah,' the corporal finally agreed, knowing that doing so was backing down and eating crow. 'I reckon we can.'

'I might accept "mister" from a man I respected,' Dusty said in that gentle, yet terribly menacing fashion his voice could adopt. 'But the likes of you call me "sir".'

'I reckon we can – sir,' Chatswen repeated, when it

became obvious that the small Texan was awaiting such a response.

'Boot those carbines and get ready to move out,' Dusty told the enlisted men. 'I've wasted too much damned time on you already.'

Glancing from side to side, Chatswen watched his men obeying with alacrity. He knew that he would receive no backing from them, even if he had contemplated taking up the small Texan's unspoken but very real challenge.

'Corporal,' Dusty said. 'I've better things to do with my time than to start asking what happened last night. There's a herd of five hundred head waiting for you. I want to hand it over and attend to more important duties.'

'Yes – sir,' Chatswen replied, hurriedly adding the honorific when Dusty frowned at its omission. 'We'll come right away, sir.'

'Just one thing, corporal,' Dusty went on. 'If I should ever hear of you pulling a game like this again, I'll have you and every man concerned transfered to my Company. And then, soldier, I'll make you wish you'd never been born.'

Staring at the *big* young blond, Chatswen and the other enlisted men knew that they were hearing a warning which it would pay them to heed. There was no bombast in the officer's voice, only a chillingly menacing promise. Something warned them that he might have the necessary influence to carry out his threat. A variety of throbbing aches, caused by the injuries inflicted in the fight, gave emphasis to their belief that service under his command would be anything but pleasant. Certainly it would be far more hazardous and harder work than their present occupations.

'Yes, sir,' Chatswen muttered, making the only comment he felt would be appropriate, acceptable, or safe, under the circumstances.

Watching the incident, Billy Jack refrained from showing the delight he was feeling. Unless he missed his guess, Mr. Fog was going to turn out as good an officer as his father. While still inexperienced, he had already displayed a sound knowledge of how to handle men.

Many young officers, faced with Mr. Fog's predicament, might have been at a loss to figure out what to do for the best. It would have been all too easy for him to have gone about handling Chatswen's bunch in the wrong manner. He could have tried to use his insignias of rank and the powers which he imagined were automatically granted to him by the *Manual of Field Regulations*, expecting them to ensure the soldiers' obedience.

Realizing just how little actual authority the *Manual of Field Regulations* and his badges of rank gave to a very young, newly appointed lieutenant – especially when dealing with men who did not belong to his regiment – Mr. Fog had guessed correctly that he must depend upon the strength of his personality.

Instead of attempting to pull rank, the small Texan had faced the recalcitrant soldiers while dressed as a civilian. He had then established a physical superiority – which they could appreciate and understand far better than any display of *Manual*-backed attempts at authority – in no uncertain manner. What was more, he had been aware that his victims might wish to take the matter even further. So he had arranged for them to witness his expert handling of firearms and had averted what might easily have ended in gunsmoke and corpses.

Although satisfied with Dusty's potential as an officer and a leader, Billy Jack still experienced misgivings regarding Red Blaze.

The red-head was brave enough, tough and a good hand in a fist fight; but he was also reckless and more than a mite foolhardy. That had been proven by the way he had changed Mr. Fog's plans for dealing with Chatswen. By disregarding his cousin's arrangements, Mr. Blaze might have caused them to become the victims, instead of them emerging as the victors.

Such a failure would have lessened, if it had not completely destroyed, any chance of the pair becoming effective officers. Once the story of their failure had made the rounds, it would have been difficult – maybe even impossible – for them to earn the respect of the Texas Light Cavalry's hard-bitten veterans.

So Billy Jack considered that Mr. Blaze would need far longer than Mr. Fog to develop into a satisfactory officer. The red-head would probably come to be well liked, but he would need to mature before he was respected and accepted as a leader. Perhaps, the sergeant told himself – and, for once, his regret was genuine – Mr. Blaze would never make it.

CHAPTER FIVE

'COLONEL BLAZE allowed's I should come and fetch—' Sergeant Billy Jack began as he rode with Lieutenants Fog and Blaze towards the herd of cattle. Then he revised his words into a more tactful form. 'I should tell you he wants the recruits getting to the regiment as fast as possible.'

'You near on said, "I should come and fetch you pair, so's you don't get lost",' Red grinned.

'Now that wouldn't've been polite of me, Mr. Blaze,' the lanky sergeant protested. 'Which I'm allus *real* polite to anybody's out-ranks me.'

'Even to green shavetails?' Dusty inquired.

'*Especially* to green shavetails, sir,' Billy Jack affirmed. 'That's 'cause I'm a good, loyal soldier – and scared they'd get mean and have me busted if I wasn't polite to them.'

Throwing a glance at his cousin, Dusty could see that Red was aware of the tribute being paid to them. By answering in such a manner, Billy Jack was showing his respect and approval.

During the ride from Arkadelphia. Dusty Fog had continued to impress Billy Jack with his potential for making an officer. With Chatswen's detail following about a hundred yards to their rear, the three Texans had talked as they kept their mounts moving at a steady trot. All the questions asked by Dusty had been to the point and showed that he possessed a fair appreciation of the conditions prevailing at that time in Arkansas.

From general matters, Dusty had turned the conversation to the Texas Light Cavalry and, in particular, Company 'C'. At first he had restricted himself to tactical duties, with Red injecting questions regarding the possibility of frequently 'locking horns with the Yankees'. After listening to some of the usual enlisted men's grouches, Dusty had drawn Billy Jack into commenting upon the man who would be his immediate superior.

With a frankness which surprised him, when he came to consider it later, Billy Jack had described Captain Otto von Hertz's character and personality.

'I surely hopes's how you young gents've got uniforms just like it says in the *Manual of Dress Regulations*,' the sergeant had said, after stating that von Hertz was a stickler for discipline, military protocol – although he did not use those exact words – and training, but also well-versed in all aspects of cavalry warfare.

'That we have,' Red had admitted wryly. 'The collar on my jacket's like to cut my head off under my chin, way it is when it's fastened.'

'You'll have to take a chance that it don't happen and keep it fastened, Mr. Blaze,' Billy Jack had warned. 'Cause that's how Cap'n von Hertz wants it.'

'Your gunbelt and saddle's not *Regulation*, sergeant,' Dusty had pointed out.

'I ain't gainsaying it, sir,' Billy Jack had replied. 'But that's only 'cause we don't have enough of the *Regulation* kind, and the cap'n's not happy about it.'

'Looks like we'll be able to go on wearing our belts, Cousin Dusty,' Red had announced, showing satisfaction until Billy Jack had demolished it.

'I wouldn't count on that, Mr. Blaze,' the sergeant had said. 'He'll expect you-all, being officers 'n' gentlemen, to wear the right kind of belts even if you don't sit McClellan saddles.'

'Whee-dogie!' Red had ejaculated. 'I can see me and Cap'n Hertz—'

'Captain *von* Hertz,' Billy Jack had corrected. 'He's tolerable set on having folks use that there "*von*", whatever it be.'

'Well all right,' Red had grinned. 'I can't see Captain *von Hertz* and me getting on too good unless one of us changes our ways. Which I'm too old, ornery and set in 'em for it to be me.'

That and similar cheerfully irrelevant remarks had done little to make Billy Jack revise his opinion regarding Red's possibilities as an officer. From other parts of the conversation, it had become obvious that the red-head hero-worshipped his smaller cousin and was satisfied that Dusty Fog could do no wrong. In fact, Billy Jack had guesed that it was Red's blind faith in the small Texan's capability, as much as a genuine enjoyment of being involved in a fight, which had led him to revise the plan for dealing with Chatswen's detail at the hotel.

Billy Jack noticed, as they drew nearer to the herd, that its bed-ground had been selected with care and showed a shrewd appreciation of the kind of precautions required to ensure its safety.

The cattle were being held close to the banks of a small stream, in a location which offered them water and good grazing. With those needs filled so adequately, they would settle down and show less inclination towards drifting away. The nearest clump of trees was at least half a mile away and there were neither ravines nor draws – that might harbour and conceal wild animals or hostile human beings – close by. Any attempt at stealing, or merely stampeding, the five hundred head of half-wild longhorn steers would have been detected and countered before it could have been put into effect, even during the night.

A corporal and four soldiers, wearing the uniforms of the Texas Light Cavalry were riding herd on the cattle. According to Dusty, there had been eight men on duty through the hours of darkness, positioned so that nobody could have approached the herd without being seen or heard. Until that morning, all such work had been carried out in civilian clothing. Wishing to avoid any further delays in joining the regiment, Dusty had ordered the change to military attire so that his party would be ready to move off as soon as they had turned the herd over to the men from the Commissary General's Department.

Galloping up, the corporal saluted Dusty and reported that everything was satisfactory with the herd. He had a bruised face and threw a scowl towards Chatswen's detail. However, it changed to a more cheerful look as he observed the burly non-com's equally battered features.

Telling Red to attend to handing over the herd, Dusty accompanied Billy Jack to the recruits' camp. Everything had been made ready for them to resume their journey. The young soldiers' gear was packed, their horses saddled and standing ground-hitched ready to be mounted. A team was hitched to the chuck wagon and the fire had been doused. There was none of the litter all too often seen when a soldiers' camp was being broken up.

Looking about him, Billy Jack could find no fault with the location of the camp-site. It was on the bank of the stream, about a quarter of a mile above the herd and between the cattle and the nearest clump of trees. At that distance, the soldiers would not have needed to worry about the normal camp's noises spooking the steers, but could have reached the animals swiftly in an emergency. All in all, it gave the sergeant yet another example of Mr. Fog's competence.

Turning his head to make some comment to the small Texan, Billy Jack found that he was looking at a horse that was tied by its reins to the chuck wagon's tailgate. The sergeant had noticed the animal, mainly because it was not with the others and apparently needed securing to something instead of being prevented from straying by merely having its reins dangling free.

Now that Billy Jack's attention had been drawn to the horse, a big roan gelding, he detected other differences.

Obviously the recruits had fetched along their own mounts on enlistment. The ground-hitched animals were typically range-bred stock. Not one topped fifteen hands and the majority lacked four inches of that height, but they looked agile, wiry, packed with vitality and endurance. Each carried a low horned, double girthed – a Texan rarely used the word 'cinch' because of its Spanish connotations – saddle with a sabre and coiled rope dangling from it.

Bigger, more powerful, the roan by the chuck wagon had one piece reins and not the two separate strands mostly used by Texans. Its light, high-horned saddle had a centrally-fitted girth and the leathers of the covered stirrups passed over the seat. No self-respecting son of the Lone Star State would be caught sitting such a Spanish-looking saddle.

Only one of the recruits was in sight. Lounging with a shoulder against the side of the wagon, he was tall, lean, with a hard, savage, Indian-dark cast of features that suggested mixed blood. As Dusty and Billy Jack rode up, he straightened and spoke over his shoulder.

Going closer, the sergeant discovered that the remainder of the party were beyond the wagon, gathered around a tall, black-clad civilian. However, at the dark soldier's words, a good-looking, sandy-haired youngster – whose sleeves bore the chevrons of a corporal – swung away from his companions. His blackened left eye, swollen top lip and bruised right cheek implied that he had been the second of Chatswen's victims. Billy Jack noticed that he did not appear to be surprised, on glancing towards the herd, to find that Mr. Fog had succeeded in returning with its new attendants. Halting as Dusty and Billy Jack dismounted, he threw up a smart salute.

'Everything's ready for us to pull out, Mr. Fog,' the corporal stated, then nodded towards the cattle. 'He allowed he'd come, happen you went for him.'

'Why sure,' Dusty agreed. 'This here's Sergeant Billy Jack. He'll be showing us the way to the regiment. Sergeant, let me present Corporal Sandy McGraw.'

'Howdy, corporal,' Billy Jack responded, extending his right hand.

'Glad to know you, sergeant,' Sandy McGraw replied.

'Who's the caller?' Dusty inquired, after they had shaken hands.

'The Reverend Hotchkiss, from Arkadelphia,' Sandy answered. 'He just now rode up and wants for us to go to some prayer meeting he's holding in town tonight.'

'What did you tell him?' Dusty asked.

'That he'd have to wait until you came back for an answer,' Sandy replied.

Before any more could be said, the civilian had turned and was walking away from the soldiers. He would not be more than in his late thirties and had a tanned, unsmiling face under a round-topped black hat of the style much favoured by preachers of various denominations. His jacket, vest, shirt, cravat and trousers were pretty much what a small town's parson might wear. Even his Wellington leg-boots were not unexpected, or unusual, items of attire. He most likely visited the country-dwelling members of his flock on horseback. However, he walked with a slightly swaggering gait that would have seemed more natural in a cavalry soldier than a man of the cloth.

'Good day, sergeant,' greeted the civilian, in a Southern but not an Arkansas' drawl. He had given Dusty just one quick glance before devoting his attention to Billy Jack. 'You've a fine body of young men here. Has your officer stayed out at the herd?'

'Nope,' Billy Jack replied, looking and sounding at his most miserable and dejected as he stared at the speaker. 'This here's Lieutenant Fog.'

Following the direction indicated by the sergeant, the civilian gave Dusty a much longer scrutiny. Hotchkiss seemed unwilling to believe his ears. Studying the excellent condition of the camp, he frowned in a puzzled manner as if unable to reconcile such evidence of discipline with the short, insignificant figure in the dress of a working cowhand. Then he swung a glance at Billy Jack, but found no enlightenment in the lanky sergeant's appearance. Once more his eyes returned to Dusty and he realized that he was not acting in a polite, or even tactful manner.

'I'm sorry, Mr. Fog,' the civilian said. 'I didn't realize who you were. My name's Hotchkiss and I've come to extend an invitation for you and your men to attend a little prayer meeting and social evening we're holding in town tonight.'

'You-all must've took over from the regular preacher real recent, Mr. Hotchkiss,' Billy Jack injected.

'I haven't taken over officially as yet, sergeant,' the civilian replied. 'But I'm the Reverend Deane's nephew and he's asked me to replace him when he retires at the end of the month.'

'I hadn't heard he was retiring,' Billy Jack stated, being puzzled by the other's appearance.

'It's not been announced yet,' Hotchkiss answered evenly. 'But he's wanting to quit. His health isn't too good.' With that, he looked pointedly away from his interrogator. 'Can I expect you and your men tonight, Mr. Fog?'

'Well now, sir,' Dusty said hesitantly, glancing at Billy Jack as if seeking approval and advice. When none came, he continued, "I'm sorry, but we won't be able to come. Will we, sergeant?'

'Nope,' Billy Jack agreed, surprised by the change which had come over the small Texan.

'May I ask why not?' Hotchkiss said, addressing Dusty.

'We'll be moving out as soon as I've changed my clothes, sir,' Dusty explained. 'Serg – I'll be starting as soon as I'm back in uniform.'

Watching Dusty, Billy Jack was at a loss to understand the way in which his confident manner had changed. He seemed uncertain and anything but the competent young officer who had so impressed the sergeant during the ride from town.

'Ah yes,' Hotchkiss said, nodding his head. 'You'll be moving the cattle again.'

'Not us, sir,' Dusty corrected. 'I've done my part of the delivery. Men from the Commissary General's Department are looking to them now.'

'Surely that leaves you free to bring your men to the meeting?' Hotchkiss stated. 'The town's ladies would be delighted to see you and your voices would be of great assistance in the hymn-singing.'

'I'm sorry, sir,' Dusty insisted, having thrown another swift look at Billy Jack. 'My orders are to get to my regiment as quickly as possible. I hope to be fifteen miles closer to Little Rock by nightfall.'

'The cattle couldn't cover that much distance, could they?' Hotchkiss asked.

'No, sir,' Dusty admitted. 'But there's no reason why they should.'

'You won't be escorting them any further?'

'Not us, sir. They're headed for our main supply depot at Pine Bluff.'

'Without your party to guard them?' Hotchkiss said, sounding puzzled.

'Shucks, sir,' Dusty affirmed. 'There's no need for us, or anybody else, to guard them. The Yankees wouldn't dare to come this far behind our lines. Corporal Chatswen's got five good men to help him and we'd be wasting our time if we went along.'

Although Billy Jack did not show it, he was growing alarmed and concerned by the trend of the conversation. As it had progressed, Mr. Fog had started to diminish in the sergeant's estimation. After having observed what he had believed to be so many sterling qualities in the small Texan, it was disappointing to hear him speaking to a stranger in such a frank, indiscreet even, fashion. Especially after Billy Jack had given an oblique warning that the civilian was not the regular preacher from Arkadelphia.

There was something about Hotchkiss that disturbed Billy Jack. It was not just his claim to be a preacher, but something deeper. Perhaps it was his bearing and attitude, or the hard look about the tanned face. None of them suggested that he was a man of peace, or the kind who would be content to stagnate in a small town like Arkadelphia. He would, Billy Jack considered, be more likely to try to take an active part in the War.

What if Hotchkiss should be taking a more active part in the War – but on the side of the Union?

Both the North and the South made use of spies in the other's territory, or so Billy Jack had heard. There could hardly be a better way for one to conceal his identity than by acting as the preacher in a small town. Such a man would be almost above suspicion and was ideally situated to obtain information. The frank way in which Mr. Fog had answered Hotchkiss's questions had been proof of the latter point.

'Sergeant,' Dusty said, cutting through Billy Jack's thoughts. 'Go and make sure everything's ready for us to move out.'

'Yo!' the sergeant replied. 'Maybe—.'

'Do I have to have every order debated?' Dusty yelped, sounding more like an indignant schoolboy whose assumed authority was challenged than the capable young officer who had dealt with Chatswen's detail.

'No, sir,' Billy Jack said, barely concealing his annoyance. 'You don't.'

'Wait here, San – corporal,' Dusty said, as Sandy made as if to follow Billy Jack. Then he looked at Hotchkiss and smiled. 'I reckon I could think up a good reason for us to stay and attend your meeting, sir.'

Alarm and disappointment showed on Sandy's face. Not only was he eager to reach the Texas Light Cavalry, attending a church social was hardly his idea of how to spend a night in town. The emotions changed to surprise. He had sensed that the sergeant disapproved of Mr. Fog for some reason and suddenly realized what had caused it. However, having known the small Texan for longer than Billy Jack had, Sandy had developed considerable faith in his judgment. If Mr. Fog allowed that the preacher was all right, Sandy accepted his summation without question. For all that, the offer he had just heard came as a surprise.

'Wouldn't that be contrary to your orders?' Hotchkiss asked, showing less enthusiasm than Sandy would have expected.

'Well—' Dusty said hesitantly. 'Well, sort of—'

'A lot more than just "sort of", I'd say,' Hotchkiss interrupted sternly.

'Shucks,' Dusty answered, lowering his head and shuffling his feet. 'We wouldn't be missed and I'd think up some story for why we were late arriving.'

'I couldn't permit *that*!' Hotchkiss declared. 'It would be almost like starting out on a lie. When I came here, I didn't realize the urgency of your orders. If I had known, I wouldn't have invited you.'

'It'd work out all right, sir—,' Dusty began.

'Whether it would or not, I can't let it happen,' protested the civilian. 'And it wouldn't do me any good for my congregation to know I'd allowed you to go against your orders.'

'You're right, I reckon,' Dusty admitted, a trifle sulkily.

'You *know* I am,' Hotchkiss barked. 'Perhaps we'll be able to entertain you and your men at a later date, when you'll be free to come. Until then, I'll wish you a safe journey to Pine Bluff!'

'Little Rock, sir,' Dusty corrected. 'It's the herd that's headed for Pine Bluff. Can I offer you a meal, or anything, sir?'

'No, thank you,' Hotchkiss refused. 'I won't do anything to delay you. Good afternoon, Mr. Fog, corporal. I wish you both every success for the future. Remember, always fight the good fight and the Lord will be strong for you.'

'I'll do just that, sir,' Dusty promised. '*Adios!*'

Still feeling puzzled and a mite annoyed by what he regarded as Mr. Fog's failure to maintain the high standard of capability, Billy Jack watched Hotchkiss walk towards the chuck wagon. Unfastening the big roan's reins, the man swung into the saddle and rode away.

Frowning, Billy Jack wondered if he should not have insisted upon continuing questioning Hotchkiss, or have demanded proof of his identity. Then he thought that maybe he was allowing his disappointment in Mr. Fog to cause his imagination to run away with him. Certainly the preacher in Arkadelphia was an old man and could be figuring on retiring. In which case, he was likely to try to have a deserving kinsman come to replace him. Yet Hotchkiss had not seemed all he should be and he could sure ride a horse real well.

Thinking back to the conversation during the ride from town, Billy Jack recollected having told Mr. Fog, on being asked, that the Yankees had never tried to interfere with the herds of cattle. There did not seem to be any reason why they should be starting right now.

Billy Jack decided that there was nothing to worry over. However, he figured that he had better warn Mr. Fog about the dangers of talking so freely with strangers. It was a pity that the young officer should have made such a potentially dangerous mistake after having behaved so admirably up to then. At least, Billy Jack consoled himself, there had been no real harm done by the small Texan's indiscretion.

Urging his horse to a trot, Hotchkiss headed towards the herd of cattle. After he had covered about a hundred yards, he shook his head in amused disgust.

'That stupid peckerwood* son-of-a-bitch,' the black-dressed man said to himself, thinking of the way in which the small Texan had given him all the information he would require. 'It looks like we're not the only Army that gives commissions to fool kids because their folks know somebody important. I almost wish he was going with the herd, so that he could see how easy he's made things for us when we take it.'

* Peckerwood: derogatory name for a Confederate supporter.

CHAPTER SIX

As Captain Stratford Hotchkiss rode through the darkness towards the camp of the men who were now handling the herd of cattle, he was still feeling amused by the ease with which he had tricked the small Texan into helping him. The information that he had been given was of the greatest value. It was making his assignment so much easier than he had hoped might happen.

When Sergeant Leps had returned from making a scout the previous night, telling how adequately the cattle were being watched over and protected, Hotchkiss had wondered if he could carry out his attempt to take them from the Rebels. Clearly somebody with the escort had known the most suitable precautions to take against such an eventuality.

Deciding to discover the strength and weakness of the escort, Hotchkiss had visited their camp. His mission was being undertaken in civilian clothing and he had along attire suitable for him to pose as a preacher from Arkadelphia. Fortunately, he had discovered the name of the town's real preacher. At first, he had doubted that he would learn anything. The smart, alert young soldiers and the condition of the camp had hinted at experienced leadership of a high quality.

Only that skinny-gutted, miserable-looking sergeant had not accepted Hotchkiss as being genuine. He was either suspicious, or more careful than his immediate superior. For a time Hotchkiss had been uneasy, for he knew nothing more about the Reverend Deane than the name and his age. However, the small luff had had to assert his authority and sent away the man who might have spoiled things for Hotchkiss. After that, the ease with which the short-grown runt had supplied all the necessary information – including the size and destination of escort *and* the name and rank of the man commanding it – had come almost as an anti-climax.

For a moment, as had happened more than once since leaving the Rebels' camp, Hotchkiss found himself wondering who had been responsible for its excellent condition. Most likely it had been the lean sergeant, whom Hotchkiss suspected of being more capable than showed on the surface. The efforts of more than one enterprising and efficient soldier had been brought to nothing by the incompetence of superiors who owed their ranks to family influence rather than ability. Hotchkiss himself was, he felt, a case in point.

Having learned something about handling cattle in California, before volunteering to serve in the Union Army, Hotchkiss had seen an opportunity to put his specialized knowledge to good use.

Sent to the Army of Arkansas, Hotchkiss had found it poorly fed and demoralized. It was not a fighting force to inspire an ambitious man with confidence or hopes for a distinguished future. Then he had seen what he had believed was a good way to gain acclaim and draw attention his way. Learning that the Rebels received regular supplies of fresh beef from Texas, he had proposed that he was given men to raid and drive the cattle back to his own lines. By doing so, he would produce food for the soldiers and cause the Confederate States' Army to use men to guard the future deliveries.

Like many another man, Hotchkiss discovered that it was easier to think up a plan than to gain acceptance and official backing for it. His own colonel and General Culver had been interested, but neither was willing openly to associate himself with something that might easily fail. However, he had received grudging and qualified permission to proceed. To his annoyance, he had been compelled to use men from his own Company instead of gathering skilled help. He had selected a sergeant and eight enlisted men with farming backgrounds. While they had not had experience with trail driving, they at least know how to handle cattle.

Helped by the information so stupidly given to him, Hotchkiss was for the first time confident of success. Once he had captured and delivered the herd, he could hope for promotion and to be given a much larger, more experienced, force with which to expand his efforts.

'Looks like they've set up camp in the bushes along by the river,' Sergeant Leps remarked, pointing ahead as his horse came alongside the roan. 'That's something we hadn't figured on.'

'It won't make too much difference,' Hotchkiss replied. 'Drop back and make sure the men know I don't want any shooting. It could spook the herd and start a stampede.'

'Sneaking up on them fellers won't be easy among the bushes,' Leps objected, instead of obeying. 'We could go straight to the herd—.'

'And have the rest of the men come after and hit us, or go to Arkadelphia for help?' Hotchkiss scoffed. 'Well do it *my* way, *sergeant*. Ride up and take the men at the fire prisoner, then go along and get the night herders. That way, the Rebs won't know what's happened until the cattle don't arrive at Pine Bluff. By that time, we'll be well on our way to safety.'

'What if them fellers don't hold with your notion about no shooting?' Leps inquired.

'Let me worry about *that*, sergeant!' Hotchkiss growled. 'Go tell the men my orders.'

'Yo!' Leps answered sullenly and slowed his horse to let the rest of the party catch up.

Hotchkiss felt irritated and annoyed by his sergeant's attitude. A career soldier, Leps had little faith in the abilities of volunteer officers. He had been openly, or covertly, critical of every decision made by Hotchkiss since the start of the mission. Much of the mistrust had arisen from Hotchkiss's reticence and reluctance to take his subordinates into his confidence. Instead of telling the sergeant all his plan, he had merely given the necessary orders and reserved several vital details until they could be produced at the most advantageous moment. By doing so, he hoped to impress the men with his brilliance.

They were drawing closer to the bushes and Hotchkiss could hear the muted, startled comments from the enlisted men as Leps passed on his orders. Stopping his horse, Hotchkiss allowed the others to catch up. There was sufficient light from the stars for him to see that they were uneasy and alarmed.

'I don't reckon we can sneak up on them fellers without 'em hearing us, cap'n,' one of the privates declared, speaking quietly, and the others muttered their agreement.

'Neither do I,' Hotchkiss admitted. 'So we're not going to try.' With that he raised his voice. 'Hello the fire. Is that you, Corporal Chatswen?'

Exclamations of consternation rose from the soldiers, but the instincts for self-preservation caused them to be held down to little more than alarmed whispers. Ignoring the *sotto voce* comments, Hotchkiss held his breath in eager – and anxious – anticipation. The answer came with gratifying promptitude and suggested that he had guessed correctly when planning his moves.

'Yeah. It's me. Who're you?'

'The Reverend Hotchkiss, from Arkadelphia. I spoke to you at the herd this morning.'

'Oh sure, I remember,' called back the voice from amongst the bushes. 'You wanting something, Reverend?'

'The ladies suggested that, as you couldn't come to our meeting and they'd cooked extra food, we should fetch it out to you,' Hotchkiss replied and the low-spoken expressions of delight which came from his men were like music to his ears. They were now suitably impressed by him. 'May we bring it?'

'Fetch it ahead, Reverend,' offered the speaker.

'Remember, men!' Hotchkiss hissed. 'No shooting. Not that there's likely to be any need for it. We'll take the peckerwood bastards by surprise.'

Having delivered his statement, Hotchkiss set the roan into motion. He grinned in delight, satisfied that he had created the desired impression upon his men. After this, they would be more responsive and willing to carry out his orders without hesitation.

'Dismount!' Hotchkiss hissed, on reaching the fringe of the bushes. 'Millet, Dorst, stay with the horses. The rest of you, have your revolvers out but keep them hidden behind your backs.'

The men obeyed with a willing speed that had rarely been in evidence when previously responding to his orders. All could see the wisdom of completing the approach to the camp on foot. The horses would be a hindrance when it came to dealing with the Rebels.

Dismounting, they passed their reins to the designated pair and followed Hotchkiss into the bushes. As they moved forward, their admiration for their officer increased with every step. There was something satisfying about being able to advance boldly and have no worries over making noises that could alert and alarm an unsuspecting camp.

'Get into line once we're in the clearing,' Hotchkiss ordered in a whisper. 'And don't show your guns until I fetch mine out.'

'Sure, cap'n,' Leps hissed back and the others gave soft-spoken agreement.

Peering ahead, the men saw that their victims had made camp in a small clearing. Four Confederate soldiers were standing by the fire, facing the oncoming party but not holding weapons. Beyond them was a chuck wagon. Its team had been unhitched and was nowhere in sight. Nor, if it came to that, were the quartet's mounts. However, none of Hotchkiss's party attached any significance to the missing animals. They were all too eager to carry out their work to pay attention to apparently unimportant trifles. Each held his revolver behind his back and thought complacently of the surprise they were going to hand to their enemies.

'Good evening, gentlemen,' Hotchkiss greeted, stepping into the clearing.

'Howdy, Reverend,' Corporal Chatswen replied, but he seemed to be nervous and his eyes flickered from side to side. 'Come ahead.'

Slowing his pace, Hotchkiss allowed his men to spread into a line on either side of him. He continued to approach the fire without producing his weapon, wanting to be so close when he did that the Rebels would realize any resistance would be fatal.

Studying the four Confederate soldiers, Sergeant Leps felt a vague, disturbing sensation creeping through him. He began to realize that there was something wrong with their attitudes. They seemed strained and did not look like men awaiting a pleasant meal. What was more, every one of them kept darting glances at the bushes as if expecting to see something – or somebody.

It was some*body*!

Figures stepped swiftly from the bushes, with revolvers or Enfield carbines lining towards the Yankees. Young men wearing cadet-grey uniforms and the silver star-in-the-circle hat badges of the Texas Light Cavalry. A tall, lean, miserable-faced sergeant and a short, young first lieutenant sprang from either end of the wagon, alighting with a revolver in each hand.

That the four men by the fire had been expecting the others was proven by the rapidity of their movements. They flung themselves to the ground, leaving the newcomers a clear field of fire at the Yankees.

'Howdy, Reverend Hotchkiss,' greeted the lieutenant. 'It looks like we've got together for that meeting after all. We'll start by having you and your deacons dropping the guns.'

For a moment Hotchkiss stood as if turned to stone. Then he felt an uncontrollable fury surging inside him. All the time he had been congratulating himself upon the ease with which he had fooled the small Texan, but it was he who had been the dupe. Somehow the young blond had suspected him and had contrived to deceive him, laying a trap into which he had walked. Not just him, either. He had brought his whole force, with the exception of the horse-holders—

'Look out, cap—!' yelled a voice from the darkness, the words ending with a thudding sound and a gurgle of agony as if the speaker had been hit hard in the pit of the stomach.

Not even the horse-holders had escaped the trap!

'You bastard!' Hotchkiss screeched – and there could be

no better description of the sound which burst from his lips – snatching his revolver into view with a reckless disregard for the consequences. 'Get them!'

Catching his superior's movements from the corner of his eye, Sergeant Leps could have quite willingly shot Hotchkiss. Up to that moment, Leps had been planning to do the sensible thing and surrender. Hotchkiss's actions were about to ruin any hope of giving up peaceably.

'Fight 'em!' Leps bellowed, bringing the Colt from behind his back.

It was a foolish gesture under the circumstances. There were fifteen Texans spaced around the clearing. Young recruits, with the exception of Billy Jack, at least half of them were armed with single-shot Enfield carbines; but they had grown up handling weapons and most had fought Indians, or bad Mexicans, at some time during their lives. So they responded to the challenge with a speed and deadly purpose that was often lacking amongst newly-enlisted men from the more civilized East.

Flame erupted from the muzzles of revolvers and carbines, while the roaring of detonated black powder shattered the silence of the night. A veritable storm of lead flew across the clearing, converging upon the Yankees as they tried to bring their weapons into action.

Hotchkiss took three bullets in the body. While his revolver was still thrusting forward and unfired, they flung him to the ground.

Struck in the head by an Enfield's solitary load, Leps twirled and fell. In going down, he sent a bullet into the ground before him. It was the only powder burned by the would-be cattle-thieves.

Four more of them took lead in the opening volley. The remainder hurriedly discarded their revolvers, raised their hands and yelled that they wished to surrender.

'Hold your fire, men!' Dusty Fog shouted, refraining from releasing the hammer of his left hand Colt as its muzzle was swung from the height of its recoil and sought for a second target.

It said much for the control the small Texan had gained over his party that they responded immediately and not another shot was fired.

Returning his Colts to their holsters, Billy Jack listened for any hint that the noise had disturbed the herd. Failing to hear anything. he concluded that he had caused it to be bedded down far enough from the camp for Mr. Blaze's detail to have no worries on that account.

'You all right, Kiowa?' the sergeant yelled.

'Why sure,' answered a voice from the direction in which Hotchkiss and his men had come. 'We got their hosses and the two fellers's was left with 'em.'

'Bueno,' Dusty replied. 'Bring them in.' Then he looked at Billy Jack. 'Sergeant, see to the prisoners. Give their revolvers to some of our men who don't own one. Do what you can for the fellers who've taken lead. Are you and your men all right, Corporal Chatswen?'

'They never touched us, lieutenant,' Chatswen declared as he and his men stood up. 'You sure called the play right all along the line, sir.'

Glancing at the burly corporal in passing to commence his duties, Billy Jack hid a grin. There had been no hesitation in Chatswen's use of the honorific that time. Then the sergeant looked briefly at Dusty and a flicker of admiration passed across his face. It changed to a wry grin as he remembered his misgivings regarding Mr. Fog's actions at the camp that morning.

When Hotchkiss had ridden away, the young officer had sent Corporal McGraw and the lean, Indian-dark soldier, Kiowa Cotton, after him. They had orders to follow him, without allowing him to see them. If he did not return to Arkadelphia, they had to learn where he was going. Then Kiowa was to keep him under observation while Sandy reported back to the camp.

Realizing that Mr. Fog was once more acting in a firm, decisive and capable manner, Billy Jack had sought enlightenment. Far from blindly accepting the visitor's story, the small Texan had been suspicious of it. The young blond had not seen Hotchkiss pass while waiting for Chatswen at the livery barn, yet he should have gone by if he had so recently come from the town. The man's bearing and California saddle had proved little, to Mr. Fog's way of thinking, but something else had been more significant. On being introduced, he had called Dusty 'Mr.', which was the correct military form of address when speaking to a lieutenant. A civilian would not have been likely to know that. Tied together, the various details had suggested to the small Texan much the same possibilities as Billy Jack had considered.

There were, the young officer had decided, objections to challenging the man's veracity. If he should be genuine, he – and many of his congregation – might deeply resent the accusation and it was important for the Army to retain the goodwill of the civilian population.

On the other hand, if Hotchkiss was a spy and planning mischief against the herd, he would not be working alone. Although he would be in custody, his companions would be at liberty to continue their schemes, or escape to their own lines. Wishing to capture the whole bunch, if possible, Mr. Fog had put on an act calculated to lull Hotchkiss into a sense of false security. He had dismissed Billy Jack in that insulting manner to prevent the sergeant from reaching the point where Hotchkiss would be compelled to produce proof of his identity. Left to himself, Mr. Fog had fed the man with sufficient information to make him think he could do his work with ease.

When Mr. Blaze and Chatswen had come to report that the herd was ready to move, they had brought news. Hotchkiss had visited them and extended an invitation for the corporal and his men to attend the prayer meeting. As such a function was of no interest to him, and knowing that Mr. Fog would not approve. Chatswen had declined. So Hotchkiss had ridden off, in the direction of Arkadelphia.

Corporal McGraw had returned, afork a lathered, hand-ridden horse, after about an hour. The news which he had brought removed any lingering doubts. Once out of sight of the herd, Hotchkiss had turned south. Unaware that he was being followed, he had joined several more men – who had also worn civilian clothing – in a wood about five miles from the town. Leaving Kiowa to keep the men under observation, Sandy had returned as fast as his horse would carry him.

On hearing the corporal's news, Chatswen had stated that the men were planning to stampede the herd. Mr. Fog had not agreed, claiming that Hotchkiss would not have taken the risks involved in visiting the camp if that was all they intended. In the small Texan's opinion – although it had never been tried by the Yankees – the men hoped to steal the herd and take it to the Union's Army of Arkansas.

Not only had the small Texan been correct in his assumption, he had proved equally accurate in deciding when and how the attempt would be made. He had figured that they would strike that night, reducing the distance they would have to drive the herd to its new destination. What was more, he had believed that Hotchkiss would want to capture Chatswen's detail, rather than having them killed from an ambush. Doing the latter might allow one or more of them to escape and fetch help and the shooting was almost certain to cause a stampede. So Mr. Fog had declared that the try would be made soon after the herd was bedded down. That would allow the Yankees to move the cattle before they had become too settled. They would also have the full night in which to take the herd around and clear of Arkadelphia; where its appearance and change of route was likely to arouse unwanted interest and attention.

Having stated his conclusions, Mr. Fog had made plans to counter the attempt. Billy Jack had changed uniforms with Japhet, who was closest amongst the herders to his lanky build, and had accompanied the cattle. The chuck wagon had been taken along, to serve as a hiding place at the night camp if it should be needed. With the cattle moving, Mr. Fog and the recruits had followed at a sufficient distance for their presence to be undetected.

The precautions had paid off when, late in the afternoon,

Billy Jack had located a man engaged in scouting the herd. When sure that the escort's proximity was unsuspected by the watcher, the sergeant had selected a camp-site and bed ground which he had felt sure was ideally suited to his officer's needs.

After keeping Hotchkiss's party under observation all day, Kiowa had slipped away when their scout – it had been Sergeant Leps – returned at sundown. Visiting the herd and camp, he had delivered a warning and gone on to report to Mr. Fog. From that point, everything had followed the small Texan's plan as if all concerned were working together.

While Mr. Blaze – complaining bitterly that his cousin was pulling rank and giving him all the worst chores – had taken some of the men to protect the herd, the remainder had moved into their places of concealment and waited for the Yankees to arrive. Nothing had been left to chance. Mr. Fog had even thought of sending away the horses so that they would not be disturbed if there should be shooting.

Shaking his head in unspoken admiration, Billy Jack thought of his conjectures regarding the young officers. No matter how Mr. Blaze turned out – and the sergeant still had doubts about him – Mr. Fog sure had the making of a leader.

''Less he gets killed off afore he gets a chance to,' Billy Jack thought, reverting to his pessimistic pose – a sure sign that he believed all was going well. 'Which he could, working with an unlucky cuss like me.'

Part Three

THE MAKING OF A LEADER, cont'd.

CHAPTER SEVEN

LEANING against his long-barrelled, muzzle-loading U.S. Model of 1861 rifle musket, Private Phineas Devlin was a bitter, disgruntled and discontented soldier. He glowered through the darkness to where three glowing areas of red light marked the camp-sites of the two infantry regiments and the large remount depot that was situated in the valley's bottom below and between them. Over there, the other enlisted men of his outfit – even those guarding the horses – were eagerly awaiting the arrival of the O'Bannion's whiskey. Back across the river, in Searcy, the officers were attending a meeting and ball, enjoying themselves while Devlin stood his lonely duty. With only that damned shavetail, Crosby, as officer of the day at the camp, the sergeant of the guard might forget to come and relieve him when his time was up; especially if the whiskey arrived and was shared out.

An annoyed snort burst from the soldier. When he had enlisted in the Chicago All-Irish Volunteers, he had expected to do more exciting things than having to stand guard at night on a bridge that crossed the Little Red River in White County, Arkansas. Yet there he was, wearing his kepi, long cloak-coat over his uniform and hung about with all the paraphernalia – a bayonet in its sheath and dangling by its frog from his waist belt, water canteen, tin cup, pack, ammunition pouches and the rest – the Army figured necessary for such a task.

At any time, even without the added inducement of the O'Bannion's gift, Devlin would have felt that the guard detail was not a fitting task for a fighting man who was ready, willing and eager to be beating the devil out of his country's enemies. It seemed even more pointless under the circumstances. What fighting was being done in Arkansas at that period was taking place a good eighty miles to the south, where the Rebels were defending Little Rock. They would never dare to come so far into Union-held territory just to destroy a bridge. So guarding it, in his opinion, was a waste of time.

'And if the guarding has to be done, why the hell couldn't they have some of them damned niggers doing it?' Devlin muttered, thinking sourly about the regiment of Negro soldiers who were camped in the vicinity.

A bitter, prejudiced man who hated coloured people – and every other racial or religious group – on principle and without thought, cause or reason, Devlin could not see why his regiment should be required to perform any duties while there were members of lesser breeds available.

The sound of a horse's hooves diverted Devlin's thoughts at the point. Turning, he stared south across the bridge to where a rider was approaching from the direction of Searcy. Although the moon had not yet come up, Devlin's eyes had grown accustomed to the darkness. In a few seconds with the rider half way across the bridge, the sentry could discern that he was a soldier of some kind.

Maybe even an officer, Devlin silently warned himself. With so many from every outfit at the meeting, there was likely to be plenty of them going back and forth before the night was through.

One thing Devlin had learned early in his brief career as a soldier was that officers always expected a man on sentry duty to act in the correct military manner. So he had better do what was expected of him.

'Halt!' Devlin shouted, bringing up the rifle to hold it at waist level and, without bothering to cock back the big side-hammer, swung its muzzle to the front. 'Who goes there?'

'Friend,' answered the rider, slowing but not stopping his large, powerful mount. He had an accent that was far different from the tall, lean soldier's broad Irish brogue. 'Easy there with that rifle, mister. It's bad enough having to ride dispatch all night without getting throwed down on every damned whichways a man turns.'

Having challenged the other soldier, Devlin found himself uncertain of what he should do next. On being posted, he had received no instructions as to his conduct. However, the response implied that the rider was not an officer and so would be willing to overlook any improper behaviour.

'Come ahead slow and easy,' Devlin ordered, although the rider was continuing to advance anyway.

Drawing nearer, the rider proved to be smallish and conveyed an impression of youth. He sat his big horse with an easy, effortless grace that would have been obvious had Devlin had experience in such matters. His right hand grasped the reins, while the left for some reason was tucked into the open front of his double-breasted cloak-coat. On his head was perched a kepi with the usual crossed sabres insignia of the U.S. Cavalry across its top. The cloak-coat concealed his tunic, but the weapon belt strapped over it appeared to be of the normal pattern. So did the sabre which dangled from the pommel of a saddle that differed in several respects from the issue McClellan; but not to Devlin's inexperienced eyes. No horseman, he failed to notice that the saddle was unlike those he had seen used by various cavalry outfits. Riding breeches and Hessian boots emerged from below the cloak-coat. Despite the darkness, Devlin could make out the yellow stripes along the legs of the breeches.

'I'd be tolerable obliged happen you'd point that rifle some other way, friend,' the rider said amiably, as the muzzle of the weapon was almost touching his mount's chest. 'Or do you reckon I'm a Johnny Reb's's come all this way behind the lines to blow up the bridge?'

Although still undecided what he should do, Devlin turned aside the rifle to avoid it striking the horse. He looked up as the rider loomed above him, left hand still hidden inside the cloak-coat. Stepping backwards a couple of paces, the sentry felt a momentary alarm. There was something wrong, but he could not decide what it might be. Then he decided that he was worrying for nothing. No Rebel would be likely to act in such a relaxed, friendly manner.

'It's only me duty I'm after doing,' Devlin pointed out, returning the butt of his rifle to the ground.

'Why sure,' answered the rider, taking his hand from the front of the cloak-coat. It emerged empty. 'I don't know which of us's got the lousiest chore, friend, you or me.'

'At least you're going some place,' Devlin commented, watching the other swing from the saddle. 'I just have to stand here. and the devil of a bit of good I'm doing. Like you said, none of 'em'd dare come this far behind our lines.'

'That's for sure,' agreed the rider, releasing his reins so that they dangled in two separate strands below the horse's bit.

Ever since the other man had replied to the challenge, Devlin had noticed the way in which he spoke. There was something about it that did not seem right. His clothes, equipment and attitude appeared correct, but the voice—

Realization struck home!

'Hey!' Devlin ejaculated, retreating a further two steps and starting to raise the rifle. 'You sound like these goober-grabber* bastards who live around these parts.'

'Easy on there, friend,' the rider protested in amiable tones. He showed no alarm other than to spread his hands clear of his sides – so that it almost looked as if he meant to slap the horse's rump with the right – and showing that they were empty. 'I'm always having this same son-of-a-bitching trouble.'

'How do you mean?' Devlin inquired.

'My folks had a ranch in North Texas and I growed up there,' the rider explained. 'Only them Secessionist bastards run us out. So I joined the Army to get back at them. And now, every time I open my mouth near on, somebody takes me for a Reb.'

*** Goober-grabber: derogatory name for a native of Arkansas.**

The sentry had not been long in the Army, but he did not wish for the smaller, younger, yet clearly more experienced soldier to realize how short his period of service had been. So he did not intend to display the uncertainty he was feeling. At the back of his mind, getting stronger all the time, was the belief that the other man could not be an enemy, no matter how he talked.

'It don't cost nothing to be careful, bucko,' Devlin commented, lowering the rifle once more and adopting what he hoped would be the tone of a seasoned veteran. 'No offence meant by it.'

'None took, friend,' drawled the rider.

'You'll likely have been in Searcy for that officers' shindig,' Devlin suggested, wanting to keep the other man talking as a means of relieving his own boredom. 'What's it all about?'

'What do you reckon it's about?' countered the other.

'I'm damned if I know,' Devlin admitted. 'All our officers, 'cepting the officer of the day's there. Same with the other outfits, I'd say.'

'It is with mine,' confirmed the rider, turning to his horse and opening its near-side saddle pouch. He removed a bottle and went on, 'I got took there to run messages. So I reckoned I was entitled to help myself to something to keep the cold out. How do you feel about soldiers drinking on duty, friend?'

'That all depends on who's doing the drinking,' Devlin answered, eyeing the bottle with considerable interest.

'My pappy allus allowed it's a mortal sin for a man to drink alone – unless there's nobody else around to take a snort with him,' the rider stated, drawing the cork. 'Here, friend, help yourself to a nip. I've already had me a couple. It's a good way to keep out the miseries on a night like this.'

If Devlin had been a more observant man, he might have noticed that the bottle was still remarkably full; considering that it was supposed to have already been sampled. Instead of seeing, he accepted it and took a long drink. The liquor burned pleasantly down his throat and made him even more determined to hold the rider in conversation, so that he might be offered other drinks.

'Now that's what I call good whiskey,' Devlin declared, wiping his mouth on his right sleeve without returning the bottle. 'The luck of the Irish to you, young feller.'

'I'm having my share of it,' thought the small horseman, conscious of the bone handled Colt 1860 Army revolver which was thrust into his breeches' waistband and pressed against his right ribs. 'And so are you. If you'd been smarter, I might've had to kill you, which wouldn't have done either of us any good.'

After only six weeks with the Texas Light Cavalry, Dusty Fog was carrying out his first independent assignment.

They had been six weeks of hard work under a demanding, but fair, superior officer and constantly watched by interested, or critical, eyes. During the period, Dusty had continued to develop his ability to control larger, older, more experienced men. He had also improved his knowledge – already obtained at Judge Blaze's small military academy – of how to carry out *caracoles*, riding and manoeuvring in echelon, or the various other cavalry drills and minor tactics.

On the whole, Dusty believed that he had acquitted himself in a satisfactory manner. In addition to earning his superiors' approbation, he had already built up a basis of trust and faith in his abilities amongst the hard-bitten veterans of Company 'C'. Billy Jack's whole-hearted support, taken with the manner of Dusty's arrival at the regiment, had been of the greatest help in achieving the latter.

For preventing the loss of the herd and capturing, or killing, every member of the Union's cattle-stealing expedition, Dusty had been allowed to retain his rank of first lieutenant. That had made him second-in-command of Company 'C'.

To an equally fortunate, but less able young officer, the appointment might have been a disastrous failure. Supported by an inborn instinct for leadership, natural intelligence and the strength of his personality, Dusty had avoided the many pitfalls that threatened a man placed in his position.

Being aware of its value, he had demonstrated his ambidextrous wizardry with the two Colts and had impressed men who were fully capable of understanding the excellence of the display. In addition, he had given convincing proof of his skill as a horse-master. On two occasions, he had been compelled to prove himself physically. Each time he had taken on a bigger, stronger, heavier man and beaten him thoroughly, yet in a way that did not humiliate the loser.

Maybe the enlisted men were not yet ready to accept Dusty as fit to command the Company in action, but he was working towards the point where – if it should become necessary – they would be likely to do so. Until then, he was satisfied with the thought that he had been considered capable of carrying out an important scouting mission.

News had reached the Texas Light Cavalry of a Union Army's remount depot having been established about ten miles north of Searcy, across the Little Red River and near to the trail to Newport, the seat of Jackson County. Even more significant, if one remembered General 'Cussing' Culber's boasts regarding the future conduct of the War in Arkansas, the Yankees were commandeering every available horse and all the fodder they could lay their hands on in the territory under their control. It all suggested that Culver was making preparations for a major offensive.

Wanting further and more definite news, Colonel Blaze had decided to send out a scouting detail. It had been Company 'C's' turn to supply the men for such a task, but Captain von Hertz was required at headquarters. So the colonel had taken the opportunity to discover how Dusty would carry out one of a cavalry officer's main duties; the gathering of information from behind the enemy's lines.

On receiving his orders, Dusty had asked for permission to select the men who would accompany him. It was granted grudgingly by von Hertz, especially when the youngster had named two of the recruits he had brought from Texas. However, as Sergeant Billy Jack and three veterans were to complete the party, the captain had agreed to the arrangement.

Having made preparations which had met with Billy Jack's approval, the party had set off. They had passed through the Yankees' forward positions at night and without difficulty. Avoiding being seen by the enemy, they had travelled towards Searcy.

During the journey, the Texans had seen two parties of Yankee officers heading in the same direction. At a ford over the Bayous des Arc River, they had watched General Culver and his staff going over, then disappearing up the trail to Searcy. Clearly something of importance was going to take place in the town.

Waiting until sundown, Dusty had allowed Billy Jack and Sandy McGraw to try to enter Searcy and see what could be learned. Sandy's uncle lived in the town, which had been the reason for Dusty asking to fetch him along. The rest of the detail had pushed on to the Little Red River. They had found the bridge was guarded. By only one man, but with the possibility of reinforcements near by. He was at the northern end, which made any chance of sneaking up on him almost impossible.

Recollecting how Hotchkiss had tried to trick him and his men, Dusty had come prepared to resort to similar methods. Apart from the colours, which were not too important before the moon rose, the Armies of the North and the South wore a similar style of uniform. The cloak-coats particularly were identical in cut and line; a point which more than one Confederate cavalry raider had turned to his advantage. Only the hats were different and Dusty had been ready to deal with that. Every member of his party had brought a U.S. Cavalry kepi, taken from Yankee prisoners and held at the regiment for just such a purpose.

For the first time, Dusty had been grateful to von Hertz for insisting that his junior officers always wore the regulation pattern gunbelt. Apart from the lettering on its buckle, it was an almost exact duplicate of the Union Army's issue. Only the saddle was different, but Dusty had gambled on it going unnoticed in the darkness and when seen by an infantryman.

Having donned the kepi, Dusty had placed the Colt where its availability was concealed. Approaching the sentry, he had been ready to draw and shoot if necessary. Or, as he had drawn nearer, had hoped to merely throw down on the man and threaten him into silence. He had managed to come close enough to make the latter feasible, without needing to do it. There had been a bad moment when the sentry had become aware of his accent, but it had passed over. However, while showing his bare hands, Dusty had been neither helpless nor harmless. If his explanation had not been accepted, he had planned to slap the horse's rump. That would have caused the high-spirited animal to bound forward. Even if it had not struck the sentry, it would have distracted him for long enough to let Dustry tackle him.

When that danger had passed, Dusty had set about the business of obtaining information. He had brought the whiskey from the regiment, figuring that it might serve the kind of purpose to which he was now putting it. He had already learned that only one officer remained at the soldier's camp and felt sure that he would be told much more if he played his cards right.

Remembering his father's comments on the way to win confidence, Dusty led Devlin to talk about his grievances. By the time the sentry had taken a couple more drinks, the small Texan knew a fair amount about the formation of the Chicago All-Irish Volunteers, the quality of its officers and non-coms, and its readiness for war. After listening to the man's grouses, Dusty turned the conversation to a matter of more immediate interest.

'What do you reckon old "Cussing" Culver's come to Searcy for?' Dusty asked, knowing that the enlisted men often picked up rumours or hints of their superiors' intentions.

'You know officers,' Devlin replied, sounding disinterested. 'They're allus getting together for one thing or another and devil the thought for the likes of you and me.'

'Some of us're figuring it might mean old "Cussing's" going to have us do what he's been telling everybody he'll do, run the Rebs back to Texas.'

'Is that the way of it, do you think?' Devlin inquired and again sampled the contents of the bottle.

'It could be,' Dusty drawled, guessing that the other had neither knowledge nor thoughts on the matter and was not especially interested.

'Well, it's not before time, if that's the way of it,' Devlin sniffed. 'Just so long as we're not expected to have to keep on doing the dirty work for them damned niggers.'

'Niggers?' Dusty repeated. 'What do you mean?'

'Aren't you with them hosses in the valley?' Devlin asked.

'Nope,' Dusty replied and continued with the answer he had decided to use in the event of such a question. 'I'm in the New Jersey Dragoons. Try another lil nip, friend.'

'It's kind you are,' Devlin stated, the words being punctuated by the call of a whip-poor-will repeated twice from the southern bank of the river. 'And it's lucky you are not to be having any truck with them niggers. *Soldiers*, they calls themselves.'

Having heard the 'bird's' call, which told him that Billy Jack and Sandy had rejoined the detail, Dusty was considering taking his departure. The moon would soon be coming up and he wanted to have his men across the river before that happened. However, the reference to Negro soldiers required investigation.

'What's up with them?' Dusty inquired.

Taking another, longer drink, Devlin launched into the required explanation. A recently formed regiment of Negro infantry had travelled West with his own outfit. From the start, there had been friction between them. In addition to resenting the Negroes' assumption of equality, the members of the All-Irish Volunteers had noticed that the coloured soldiers appeared to be better armed and equipped than themselves.

'You should see them uniforms and tents 'n' everything

they've got. And every last mother's son of 'em's got a breech-loading rifle,' Devlin continued, glaring bitterly at the weapon in his left hand. 'And good Americans like us have to make do with *these* damned things. Colonel Milligan tried to make them swap with us, but them stinking soft-shells* 's is their officers – may the Devil take them all – wouldn't let it happen. Nigger-loving bastards!'

Once more Devlin raised the bottle and the level of the whiskey sank lower. Then he continued with the catalogue of his regiment's grievances against the Negro soldiers. Not only had they been allowed to use the same kind of railway cars during the first stage of the journey from the East, but their officers had insisted that they were given the first choice in accommodation.

On their arrival in White County, the two regiments had been ordered to set up camp on opposite rims overlooking the valley along which the remount deport was established. They were there to protect the horses, but when the time had come to commence the actual guard duties, the task had fallen upon the Chicago All-Irish Volunteers.

'I'll tell you, we was riled about that,' Devlin declared. 'But their colonel's got more pull than Joe Milligan. So we have to send out a full company a night to guard the horses, while them black bastards sit on their fat butts, doing nothing. I tell you, bucko, it's sick to our guts we are of them and their uppy ways. We don't let niggers act that way back home in Chicago.'

Although Dusty was not too interested in the sentry's attitude towards the Negro soldiers, he had remained in the hope of learning something useful. Having discovered the strength of the guard at the remount depot, he decided that he had exhausted the soldier's use as a source of information.

'Well, I'd best be getting on my way,' Dusty said.

'Your bottle's near on empty,' Devlin said, sounding puzzled by such an unexpected phenomena. He had reached a state of intoxication where he felt a desire to be generous,

* Soft-shell: derogatory name for a liberal-intellectual.

especially to such a sociable, friendly companion. 'Still it's my turn to get the next.'

'Do you have it with you?' Dusty inquired, turning towards his waiting horse and reaching for its trailing, split-ended reins; another pointer to his true identity that the sentry had overlooked.

'No,' admitted Devlin. 'But I'll you what to do, bucko. Are you headed for Newport?'

'Why sure,' Dusty agreed, thinking fast to decide upon an acceptable reason for visiting that town.

It was not needed.

'Then keep your eyes open for a wagon on the trail. If there's a sergeant and three fellers with it, it'll be coming to our camp,' Devlin went on, without waiting for an explanation. 'Call in on the way back and ask for Phineas Devlin, which's me, and I'll return the favour you've done me this night.'

'I don't follow you,' Dusty said, truthfully, postponing his intention of departing although the night was growing lighter.

'Isn't it the whiskey that's been given to us by the O'Bannion – a saintly man – as's coming this night?' Devlin asked and elaborated on the statement.

Being involved in recruiting the regiment, a prominent Chicago politician had offered the inducement of a regular supply of whiskey to all who joined. Not just for the officers, Devlin insisted, but sufficient to ensure that every enlisted man had his fair share. The latest consignment was on its way south from the railroad and was due to reach the camp that night.

'I sure hope it gets here safely,' Dusty drawled, an idea starting to develop in his imaginative, fertile head.

'And why shouldn't it?' Devlin demanded indignantly.

'A wagon-load of whiskey'd be mighty tempting pickings to a lot of folks,' Dusty elaborated. 'Them niggers like to take a drink or more, I've been told.'

'Just let 'em try to touch a single bottle of the blessed stuff!' Devlin growled. 'If they did that, it's little good their officers'd do 'em.'

'All the same, it's lucky their officers haven't gone to the meeting,' Dusty remarked and received the information he had hoped for.

'But they have gone,' Devlin said, a worried note creeping into his voice. 'If I thought that—'

'There's riders coming,' Dusty interrupted, swinging astride his horse.

That had been the signal agreed upon with his men. Seeing him mount, they started to ride from their places of concealment and head towards the bridge.

'Who are they?' Devlin asked, glaring across the river.

'Look like some of our boys,' Dusty answered. 'Oh hell. Lieutenant Billy Jack's with them. I'd be obliged if you'd not mention that bottle, friend.'

'That's the way of it, huh?' Devlin grunted, setting the bottle on the ground. 'Count on good old Phineas Devlin not to let a pal down.'

'Howdy, Lieutenant!' Dusty called. 'I was just asking the sentry which's the best way to Newport.'

Without replying, Billy Jack led the others to join Dusty. Realizing his own position, Devlin stood at as steady a brace as he could manage and let the Texans ride by without speaking to them; although he gave Billy Jack a salute.

'You-all sure got promoted fast, Billy Jack,' drawled Private Kiowa Cotton as the detail passed out of hearing distance of the sentry.

'Why sure,' agreed the sergeant miserably. 'And now I'm likely to get busted again.'

'Didn't you get to see Sandy's uncle?' Dusty inquired.

'I'll have to say "no" to that,' Billy Jack confessed in his most dejected fashion.

'You're busted back to sergeant,' Dusty declared, then became serious. 'What happened?'

'Found a sign fastened to a tree outside town,' Billy Jack explained. 'It said there was a curfew from sundown and anybody seen on the streets'd be shot. Streets were alive with Yankee patrols, too. You know me, I'm fearless. But I recollected you'd said you'd's soon not have the Yankees all riled up. So I concluded we'd best come and report.'

'*Bueno*,' Dusty drawled. 'I've found that there's two new regiments been moved in here. What do you make of it, sergeant?'

'Reinforcements,' Billy Jack replied. 'Now they're here, Culver's called him a council of war and's figuring how he can run us Southron boys out of Arkansas, like he's being saying he would.'

'That's about how I see it,' Dusty conceded. 'You know, sergeant, was he to lose those remounts it'd make things a whole heap harder for him.'

'And you-all're figuring on trying to make him lose them,' Billy Jack guessed looking at the small Texan.

'Let's say I'm going to see if there's a way we can do it,' Dusty corrected. 'If we can, you might even win back your promotion.'

'With my luck,' Billy Jack wailed dismally, 'we're more likely to get seen at it, catched and killed.'

'I just knew you'd be pleasured to back my play,' Dusty declared. 'It does a man real good to know he's got such brave, trusting and willing help.'

CHAPTER EIGHT

'THERE's no way's I can see for us to get at them hosses, Mr. Fog,' Billy Jack declared miserably, as he lay alongside the small Texan amongst a clump of bushes and looking into the valley. 'With the moon up and all, we're sure to be seen by the guards.'

Behind the sergeant's mournful façade lay genuine disappointment, for he had hoped that they might be able to achieve something against the Yankees' remount depot. Certainly it was a tempting target and of sufficient importance to make the taking of risks worthwhile. Unfortunately, their examination of the area did not lead Billy Jack to believe that they could hope to succeed.

'That's for sure,' Dusty conceded. 'There'd be too many of them for us to take them all out of the deal. Not counting all the extra help they could right easy call on from the camps on the rims.'

Although there was no fence surrounding the remount depot, the six large pole corrals holding the horses were adequately covered by patrolling sentries. What was more, the few areas that would have been in deep shadow were illuminated by the fires kept blazing in basket-like iron cressets. More cressets lit up the two infantry camps and the hour was far too early for many of the soldiers to have turned into their beds. The prospects looked anything but good for the small detail of Texans.

'What're you figuring on doing now, sir?' Billy Jack asked, for his companion had not sounded perturbed or disappointed.

'We may as well go back to the others,' Dusty replied, starting to rise.

'It's sure a pity we can't scatter 'em,' the sergeant went on, throwing a look into the valley as he came to his feet. 'That'd play all hell with any notions ole "Cussing" Culver's got for doing meanness to us Southron boys.'

'Why sure,' Dusty agreed.

'Maybe Kiowa and young McGraw'll have better luck with that wagon you sent 'em to look for,' Billy Jack went on, eyeing his young officer in a quizzical manner. 'Not that I'm expecting 'em to.'

'That's more like you,' Dusty drawled, directing a final glance across the valley at the camp occupied by the Negro soldiers and turning to lead the way through the bushes. 'I was getting scared you'd had an accident and was starting to look on the bright side.'

'Any time that happens, I right soon stop it,' Billy Jack assured him. 'That way I don't get the miseries so bad when things start going wrong. Which they allus do for me.'

Withdrawing cautiously to where they had left their horses concealed in a hollow, Dusty and Billy Jack mounted. They rode away from the vicinity of the valley without being seen by anybody in either of the camps. After covering about a mile, they approached a small, but thick, grove of post oaks. Billy Jack gave a fair imitation of a whip-poor-will calling twice and received a similar answer to the pre-arranged signal. Entering the grove, they could see the glow of a small fire amongst the trees. On reaching it, they found all but one of the enlisted men standing and looking in their direction.

'How'd it go, Sandy?' Dusty inquired, leaving his bay ground-hitched.

'Well, we found a place where we *could* jump the wagon, sir,' Sandy McGraw replied. 'Kiowa send me back to tell you. He's pushed on up the trail to see if it's coming.'

'It's not too good a place, huh? Dusty asked.

'Nope,' Sandy admitted. 'But it's the *only* place anywheres along the trail for over two mile, as we could see.'

'Do'you mind if I ask what's in that wagon, Mr. Fog?' one of the veteran privates put in.

'Whiskey,' Dusty drawled.

'Whisky!' repeated the veteran and his voice took on a more hopeful timbre. 'Whee-dogie! Everybody's going to be real pleased with us, happen we can get it back to the regiment.'

'That's for sure,' agreed the second of the old hands. 'They'll all—'

'We're not going to try to take it back,' Dusty warned, not wanting his men to build up hopes that he must shatter.

'What you got in mind to do with it, sir?' the third veteran inquired.

'Give it to the Yankees,' Dusty answered, in a matter of fact fashion.

The time had not yet arrived when the small Texan could make startling, unexpected announcements and have them accepted by the veterans of Company 'C'. So the three older privates exchanged puzzled glances, then turned their eyes in an inquiring manner to Billy Jack. Sandy McGraw was just as baffled by Dusty's words but had greater faith in his judgment, and waited expectantly for him to continue with his explanation.

'There's some's might figure it's wasting time to take it away, happen all we intend to do is give it back to em, sir,' Billy Jack commented, while the three veterans muttered their agreement.

'Well, now,' Dusty said quietly. 'I wasn't exactly figuring on giving it back to the same Yankees we'll be taking it from.'

At that moment, they heard the sound of fast-moving hooves approaching.

'Sandy,' Dusty went on, giving the others no opportunity to question his last statement. 'Haul some of those branches from the fire and let the burned ends cool down. We'll need them, if Kiowa's bringing the right news.'

Once more the veterans displayed interest, but a lack of understanding. None of them had been surprised when their young officer had told them to make a fire in the centre of the grove. They knew that, in wooded country, a small fire was less likely to be seen from a distance at night than in daylight, when the smoke rising from it was noticeable.* Mr. Fog's words had implied that the fire was to serve some other purpose than making the camp more comfortable, but the veterans could not imagine what it might be.

Riding through the trees, his horse showing signs of having travelled a good distance at speed, Kiowa Cotton slipped from his saddle at the edge of the fire's glow. Dropping his reins, he slouched towards Dusty.

'It's coming, Mr. Fog,' the Indian-dark soldier announced, delivering what passed as a salute. 'Sergeant and three men riding guard, two more on the wagon. I reckon it's them. Leastwise, they all sound liquored up and Irish, way they're singing.'

'How far off are they?' Dusty wanted to know, watching Sandy drawing a couple of thick branches from the fire.

'Bout three miles, when I left 'em,' Kiowa replied. 'They're not pushing their hosses.'

'That ought to give us enough time to get everything ready,' Dusty said, half to himself. Then he turned his gaze to Billy Jack. 'Have the crossed sabres taken off those Yankee kepis, sergeant. Then I want everybody with their hands and faces black.'

'Yo!' Billy Jack agreed, but puzzlement was plain on his face.

'Tell me about this place you've got in mind for us to use when we jump the wagon, Kiowa,' Dusty requested, ignoring the muttered comments and pointed glances being directed his way as Billy Jack set the enlisted men to carrying out his order regarding the kepis.

'It's not good,' Kiowa admitted. 'But it's the only place where you could get in close enough to jump 'em, happen you're set on doing it.'

'I am,' Dusty assured him.

'It'd be easier to lay up and shoot 'em as they go by,' Kiowa pointed out. 'You couldn't get close to the trail with-

* The British Army engaged in anti-Mau-Mau terrorist patrols in the Kenya forests also took advantage of this fact.

out being seen, 'cepting at this place, but you could get to maybe a hundred yards of it.'

'I want them alive, at least some of them, if I can get them.'

'Then it'll have to be that place. There's a rise on the right of the trail, but at this place it drops straight down instead of being a slope, and the wagon has to go by along the bottom of it.'

'How high's the rim?'

'Not much higher'n the top of the wagon's cover.

'That's high enough!' Dusty enthused.

'Way the trail curves, they'd see us if we sat our hosses on the top of the wall or even back a ways from it.'

'Huh huh!' Dusty grunted. 'How're the men riding?

'Sergeant and one of them was out front, the other two flanking the wagon box, 'Kiowa replied.

'And they'd been drinking?'

'If they hadn't, they was sure trying to sound like they had.'

'*Bueno!* Dusty ejaculated and Kiowa could see that he was satisfied with what he had heard. 'I reckon we can make a stab at it.'

Wishing to avoid raising false hopes amongst his men, Dusty had kept them in ignorance of what he hoped to do until he knew that he had the means available to put the scheme into operation, Kiowa had satisfied him on that point, so he did not delay any longer before taking them into his confidence. He told them all he had learned from the sentry at the bridge and how he hoped to turn his discoveries to their advantage. Listening, the men stared at their youthful officer with a mixture of surprise and incredulity. Billy Jack, Kiowa and Sandy showed that they were interested. However, the three veteran privates were more inclined to be critical and doubtful.

'Them fellers'll see we're not Yankee infantry, even if we've got our faces and hands black,' one of the trio objected. 'Our uniforms aren't even the same colour.'

'All of the men with the wagon've been drinking,' Dusty

pointed out. 'And, happen we handle things right, it'll all be over so fast they'll not have the chance to think about how we're dressed.'

'It'll never work,' Billy Jack wailed, setting his seal of approval upon the scheme. 'We'll be seen afore they get under us. I'll bet none of us're alive comes morning.'

Watching the veterans' response to the doleful comment, Dusty was grateful for having won Billy Jack's confidence and trust. The three enlisted men looked less dubious and uncertain than they had while he was telling them of his idea. While they had been disinclined to support openly such an unconventional notion as Dusty had outlined, they had faith in their sergeant's judgment. Clearly Billy Jack considered that the scheme could work, so they were more willing to go along with it.

The preparations were made quickly. Using the charred ends of branches from the fire, the men blackened their faces and hands. While they did so, Dusty had different members of the party impersonate a coloured man's way of speaking. Selecting the most accurate, he warned them that they must sound as minstrel shows would have most likely taught men raised in the North to expect Negroes to speak. At last, wearing the unmarked kepis, but no further disguises, they mounted up and set off on their mission.

Approaching the trail, Dusty ordered his men to dismount. The horses were left in the reluctant care of the oldest veteran, while the remainder of the detail continued their advance on foot. Billy Jack, Sandy McGraw and the other two veterans each carried his coiled rope.

On reaching the top of the small cliff, Dusty could see that Kiowa had been correct in his assumption as to where an ambush would be possible. There was no other place along the trail that would have allowed them to come so close and remain undetected. Nor would there have been sufficient time for them to make hiding places. Already they could hear singing, hooves, the rumbling of wheels and creaking of leather.

Swiftly Dusty surveyed his surroundings, as he and his

men flattened on their bellies on the top of the cliff. The area was almost perfect for his needs, he decided. Below him, the wall fell perpendicular and formed the edge of the trail. Even if the wagon was at the far side, it ought to still be within leaping distance. Most likely though, with a rider on each flank, it would be travelling along the centre of the trail.

'They sure sound like they're enjoying life,' Billy Jack remarked disapprovingly, shaking loose the coils of his rope and extending its loop. 'I don't reckon they'll be too all-fired eager and watchful.'

'Or me,' Dusty agreed. 'In fact, I'm counting on just that.'

'Now me,' the sergeant declared. 'I never count on nothing going *right*.'

'Tell you what,' Dusty growled, glaring at the miserable, care-worn face. 'If you get killed because of me I'll say I'm sorry most humble.'

Despite his gloomy words, Billy Jack was studying the wagon and its escort as they came into sight. The moon was up and there was good visibility. While that would allow the Texans' blackened hands and faces to be seen clearly, it also showed all too clearly that they did not wear the uniforms of the Yankee Infantry. However, his examination of the approaching party suggested that, once again, Mr. Fog had drawn some mighty smart conclusions. If their behaviour was anything to go by, they were unlikely to be too observant.

As when Kiowa had seen them, the burly sergeant and an equally brawny private rode ahead of the wagon. The other two ranged their horses on either side of the vehicle. The sergeant and two men on the driver's box were armed with revolvers, holstered on their waist-belts, but the three mounted privates each had his long Springfield rifle resting across his knees.

'That bastard beyond the wagon's too far back for us to rope him!' Billy Jack whispered, indicating one of the pair who were riding beside the vehicle. 'You just can't trust Yankees to do nothing right.'

carded rifle. He listened to the conversation and swung his gaze to discover where he would be most usefully employed.

The sergeant and the other point rider were now seated side by side on the trail. While the former tried to free his arms, the latter clutched wildly at the rope that was threatening to strangle him. On the rim, Billy Jack and the two privates braced themselves and kept the loops tight.

Being unable to see the last rider. Kiowa ran around the rear of the wagon. Although unhorsed, partially choked and winded the Irishman had managed to land on his feet and was jerking at the rope. Hearing Kiowa approaching the man turned. In this he was hampered by his captor manipulating the rope in a way that hindered his movements. Having no room to manoeuvre Kiowa raised the borrowed rifle above his head in both hands. Down it whipped, the butt catching the soldier on the forehead. Blood gushed from the gash it caused and its recipient reeled. For a moment the rope held him erect. Slackening his grip, the Texan allowed his captive to collapse limply.

Hurdling the man's motionless body, Kiowa ran forward. He saw that Sandy had already reached the sergeant and, delivering the base of the Colt's butt in a hammer-like blow to the top of the non-com's skull, knocked him senseless.

'You have de last one, Bones!' Sandy offered, pointing to where the remaining Yankee was struggling to rise, get free, or do anything that might save him from his companions' fates.

Advancing, while the man on the rim tugged repeatedly on the rope and kept his catch off balance, Kiowa once again used the rifle's butt. He hit the Irishman behind the head and ended all the resistance – such as it had been – from the whiskey wagon's escort.

'Good going!' Dusty praised, looking around to make sure that only his own men could hear him. Satisfied that the Yankees were all unconscious, he continued with orders. 'Sergeant, get our horses up here. Kiowa, Sandy, move those two out of the way. Then get the wagon moving.'

'It worked, Mr. Fog,' Sandy enthused as he bent to remove the rope from the sergeant's neck.

'So far,' the small Texan replied. 'But we've a fair way to go yet.'

There were, Dusty realized, still things that could go wrong; but at least the first portion of his plan had been successfully accomplished.

carded rifle. He listened to the conversation and swung his gaze to discover where he would be most usefully employed.

The sergeant and the other point rider were now seated side by side on the trail. While the former tried to free his arms, the latter clutched wildly at the rope that was threatening to strangle him. On the rim, Billy Jack and the two privates braced themselves and kept the loops tight.

Being unable to see the last rider. Kiowa ran around the rear of the wagon. Although unhorsed, partially choked and winded the Irishman had managed to land on his feet and was jerking at the rope. Hearing Kiowa approaching the man turned. In this he was hampered by his captor manipulating the rope in a way that hindered his movements. Having no room to manoeuvre Kiowa raised the borrowed rifle above his head in both hands. Down it whipped, the butt catching the soldier on the forehead. Blood gushed from the gash it caused and its recipient reeled. For a moment the rope held him erect. Slackening his grip, the Texan allowed his captive to collapse limply.

Hurdling the man's motionless body, Kiowa ran forward. He saw that Sandy had already reached the sergeant and, delivering the base of the Colt's butt in a hammer-like blow to the top of the non-com's skull, knocked him senseless.

'You have de last one, Bones!' Sandy offered, pointing to where the remaining Yankee was struggling to rise, get free, or do anything that might save him from his companions' fates.

Advancing, while the man on the rim tugged repeatedly on the rope and kept his catch off balance, Kiowa once again used the rifle's butt. He hit the Irishman behind the head and ended all the resistance – such as it had been – from the whiskey wagon's escort.

'Good going!' Dusty praised, looking around to make sure that only his own men could hear him. Satisfied that the Yankees were all unconscious, he continued with orders. 'Sergeant, get our horses up here. Kiowa, Sandy, move those two out of the way. Then get the wagon moving.'

'It worked, Mr. Fog,' Sandy enthused as he bent to remove the rope from the sergeant's neck.

'So far,' the small Texan replied. 'But we've a fair way to go yet.'

There were, Dusty realized, still things that could go wrong; but at least the first portion of his plan had been successfully accomplished.

'That's for sure,' Dusty agreed. 'So you'd best leave him to Kiowa or me.'

'Yo!' the sergeant answered.

'Remember,' Dusty went on. 'We're coloured folks, but the kind those fellers've seen in minstrel shows. Talk like it.'

'Yoh-all can count on us to do des' that, Rastus,' promised one of the veterans, employing the type of accent and name used by such performers.

'I jes' hopes them white gennelmen appreciates what we-all's doing, Sambo,' Sandy McGraw stated, following his older companion's example.

'Hold the noise down!' Billy Jack hissed.

Silence fell amongst the Texans, but the precaution was not necessary. Every member of the Yankee party had clearly taken sufficient drinks to render him in a musical frame of mind. Their voices, raised in song, would have drowned louder noises than the watchers' quiet words and none of them were bothering to look around them in search of possible enemies.

Nearer came the wagon, with the sergeant and his companion leading the way with a blissful– or whisky-induced – disregard for anything other than the song they were bellowing. Quickly Dusty gave his final instructions for the attack.

Slowly, carefully, the Texans eased themselves into positions of greater readiness. Their attention flickered between the wagon, the riders and where Dusty and Kiowa were backing away from the rim.

Cautiously the small blond rose. With some relief, he discovered that he could see the top of the wagon's canopy although the riders were hidden by the edge of the cliff.

'Now!' Dusty hissed, thrusting himself into motion, with Kiowa on his heels.

Even as Billy Jack and the other men came to their feet, spaced far enough apart so that each would have room to spin and throw his rope, Dusty reached the rim and jumped. Still the Irishmen were not displaying any sign of hearing, or becoming aware of, the danger that was threatening them.

The small Texan landed on the canopy, feeling it give under his weight; but it held up against the pressure. Down came his second foot, on the other side of the centre bar, and he caught his balance deftly. A moment later, Kiowa alighted behind him with equal success.

Hearing and feeling the impacts of the two Texans' arrivals on top of the canopy, the man seated by the driver started to rise. Swaying from side to side, due to the influence of the whiskey he had consumed, he turned to investigate. Shock twisted at his face as he stared upwards to where Dusty and Kiowa loomed above him. Although the light of the moon clearly illuminated every detail of their appearances, only the colour of their skins attracted his attention and he drew the required conclusion. Like most members of the Chicago All-Irish Volunteers, he had a very prejudiced nature and outlook. Conditions during the journey had served to increase his already considerable intolerance and bias against Negroes. So he was willing to accept the newcomers at their face value, without thinking of other details.

'Niggers!' the soldier screeched.

Wishing to prevent the Irishman from noticing and realizing how the 'niggers' were clad, Dusty lashed around his right boot. Its toe thudded against the side of the man's head an instant after the word had left his lips. Already off balance, the kick completed the destruction of his equilibrium and he pitched sideways from the box.

Bringing his foot down from delivering the attack, Dusty teetered briefly before regaining his balance. He felt the canopy vibrate beneath him and heard an ear-splitting yell as Kiowa left it to deal with the horseman on the far side. At the same moment, the rest of the detail started to carry out their parts of the affair.

While Dusty and Kiowa were still in mid-air, Billy Jack was measuring with his eyes the distance separating him from his target. An expert with a rope, he had selected the rider farthest from the rim. Satisfied with his aim, he swung his rope in one fast whirl to the right and up over his head.

Then, causing the loop to flatten out horizontally, he sent it forward. It passed above the leading private and dropped neatly over the Yankee sergeant's head and shoulders. Twitching the loop tight, the lanky non-com jerked his Federal counterpart over the cantle of the saddle and dumped him rump-first on the hard ground.

'Get the white bastards!' howled Sandy McGraw, having been told to help plant the idea of Negroes being responsible for the attack and to leave the catching of the riders to the older men.

Like Billy Jack, the two veterans had been cowhands before enlisting in the Texas Light Cavalry. Each duplicated his hooley-ann throw* so well that all three ropes were in flight at the same time. Having a shorter distance to cover, the privates achieved equal accuracy. Snared around the neck, the soldier at the sergeant's side joined him in being unhorsed. Nor did the man on the near side of the wagon fare any better. Ensnared by a constricting coil of rope, he was plucked from his mount and deposited half-strangled and winded upon the trail.

Leaving Dusty to attend to the men on the box, Kiowa gave his attention to the rider who was beyond the reach of the ropers. He saw the man's head and torso swivelling in his direction and the mouth dropped open in amazement. Letting out a Kiowa war whoop, the Texan hurled himself from the wagon. Spreading apart his legs, he passed them on either side of the bewildered Irishman. Even if the other had intended to try to use his rifle, the opportunity was denied him.

Looking as if he was sitting on the man's lap, Kiowa bore him from his horse. They went down together, but Kiowa was expecting that it would happen. So he alighted on his feet and painlessly. Less fortunate, the Irishman smashed on to the unyielding surface. Nor did his troubles end there. Still straddling his victim, Kiowa let his rump descend with all his weight on to the man's chest. Although Kiowa was ready to continue his assault, he found that it was not

* A full description of the hooley-ann throw is given in *Trail Boss*.

necessary. The impact had already rendered the Yankee soldier unconscious.

Alarmed by the sudden disruption of what had been, up to that moment, a most pleasant and uneventful journey, the driver also started to stand up. Dusty did not give him the chance to do more than elevate his rump from the seat. Dropping to sit on the front arch of the canopy's support, he placed the sole of his right foot against the man's shoulder and shoved. Letting out a wail and dropping the reins of the four-horse team, the driver shot head-long from the box and sprawled downwards helplessly. Although the small Texan leapt after the man, it was not to continue the attack. Ignoring his victim, he ran to the heads of the two leading horses so as to get them under control and prevent any tendency to bolt.

Being dissatisfied with the part assigned to him, especially as he saw the other three men's ropes flying accurately and knew that he would not need to use his own, Sandy McGraw sought for another way to help. The solution was simple enough, if risky. Dropping his rope, he darted along the edge of the rim and leapt outwards.

Landing on the canopy, just after Dusty and Kiowa had quit it, Sandy slid recklessly from the top to the ground. The driver was struggling to rise and the youngster darted towards him as he shook his head in a dazed manner. Driving a kick against the man's temple, Sandy ended any danger of intervention from that source. However, a glance around showed that there were others requiring attention if the attack was to succeed.

'Get the white bastards, Rastus!' Billy Jack yelled, having watched Sandy's departure. 'Take that whiskey!'

'Ah'll do that, Sambo!' the young soldier answered, retaining sufficient presence of mind – despite his excitement – to respond in the correct fashion. He drew the 1860 Army Colt from its holster, but grasped it around the cylinder and with the butt ahead of his hand. 'Ah sure likes white fellers' whiskey!'

Leaping to his feet, Kiowa scooped up his victim's dis-

CHAPTER NINE

LEISURELY tossing pieces of wood into the cresset before the guard tent, the Negro sentry became aware of movement on the edge of the woodland some distance from the camp. Reaching for his Sharps breech-loading rifle, he looked to where a wagon emerged along the trail that led to Herber Springs. At first, he saw no cause for alarm. It was the usual type of four-horse vehicle used in considerable numbers by the Quartermaster Corps. However, he did not return to his work of feeding the fire. He enjoyed being in a position where he could order white people around; even if only to the extent of making one halt and submit to his questioning at a guard post.

Bringing his rifle into the ready position, the sentry prepared to challenge the driver. He was debating whether to make the approaching man halt the wagon some yards away, dismount and advance to be recognized, then he stared harder. Suddenly a feeling of superstitious fear bit at him. Although the four horses continued to walk towards the camp, the wagon's box was empty.

There was no driver!

'Hey, serge!' the sentry yelled. 'Come out here and take a look at this!'

'What's up?' was the reply from the guard tent.

'You come and see!' the sentry insisted.

Followed by the other occupants of the tent, a burly Negro sergeant strode out. None of them were armed and their eruption lacked any suggestion of military purpose or precision.

'What do you wan—?' the sergeant began, then he too saw the wagon. 'Now where the hell's that come from?'

'I dunno,' admitted the sentry. 'It just come along the trail with nobody driving it.'

'We'd best fetch it in,' the sergeant decided, while a low muttering rose from the man behind him. None of them moved, however, and his voice took on a harsher note. 'You heard me! Go fetch it in.'

'Looks like it's coming, fetched or not,' the sentry pointed out. 'Ain't no call to go and meet it.'

'I ain't in this man's Army to go fetching no wagon,' stated another of the guard, as the sergeant's eyes swung in his direction. 'Especially when they comes from nowhere, without nobody driving them.'

Seeing the lights of the camp, the experienced horses sensed that their hard day's work might soon be ended. So they kept walking towards the soldiers.

'Maybe we should get the officer-of-the-day,' suggested a third enlisted man, sensing that he might be called up to go near the mysterious wagon. 'Him being so well eddicated 'n' all, he'll know for sure what to do.'

'Where the hell is he?' demanded the sergeant, seeing that he might be able to pass the buck to his superior.

'He went down the valley,' supplied the sentry. 'Allowed that, with all their officers likely in town for the meeting, he'd best go and make sure them Mick-landers's doing their work properly. He reckons they's all likely to be sleeping if he don't watch 'em.'

None of the men thought it unusual that their officer-of-the-day should take it upon himself to check on the behaviour of the Irish sentries, nor that he would inform one of their number of his suspicions. As an aid to winning the Negroes' confidence, their officers invariably spoke disparagingly about the abilities and trustworthy qualities of white soldiers. So, although the officer-of-the-day was only accepting an invitation to have supper with his opposite number at the remount depot, he could not resist the opportunity to ingratiate himself with one of his men.

'What're we going to do about that thing, serge?' a soldier wanted to know.

The question posed a problem for its recipient. In their desire to 'prove' their beliefs in racial equality, the officers had taken their Negro sergeant major and carefully selected sergeants to the meeting in Searcy. Wishing to create a good impression, they had picked all the most responsible and capable of the non-coms. So the sergeant had nobody to whom he could turn for guidance, or who would have given the correct advice if he had asked for it. He held his own rank more on muscular prowess than intelligence or military knowledge.

While the men had been talking and the sergeant was trying to reach a decision, the wagon had continued to draw nearer. Studying it, the sergeant became aware that the reins were fastened to the brake's handle. A moment later, he noticed something familiar standing on the otherwise unoccupied box. Stepping forward, he reached towards the head of the near-side lead horse. The tired animals came to a stop. Striding by them, he detected an aroma which he identified.

'It was spirits's caused this to come here,' the sergeant announced, reaching over to take the bottle of whiskey from the driver's seat. 'But they was this kind.'

'How d'you mean,' asked the sentry, still eyeing the wagon warily.

'The driver's likely been guzzling this and fell off,' the sergeant explained, drawing the cork from the bottle and taking a long drink. 'Yes sir. I'll bet that's all's's happened.'

'Is that for-real whiskey?' the sentry inquired hopefully.

'Well now,' answered the sergeant. 'I'll just take another pull to make sure of it.'

'I'll help you make sure,' offered a soldier, running the tip of his tongue over his lips. 'Happen you're so minded.'

'Wonder what's in that wagon,' another went on, when the sergeant declined to reply.

'Take a look and find out,' suggested a third.

For a moment nobody offered to follow the suggestion. Then curiosity overrode the sentry's superstitious awe.

Resting the rifle against the side of the wagon, he scrambled on to the box. There was sufficient light from the cresset for him to see inside. The interior was packed with boxes and he was not left in doubt as to some of their contents. Several at the front had had their tops removed. He could see that they were filled with bottles or jugs of the kind used for holding whiskey.

'Look at these!' the sentry whooped, turning with a bottle in each hand. 'It's full of 'em, boys.'

Excited comments arose from the rest of the guard. Jumping to the ground, the sentry passed one bottle to a friend and opened the other.

'Maybe you'd best let me try it, Ben,' hinted the man who had offered to help the sergeant.

'You get your own,' the sentry replied. 'There's plenty more where this come from.'

'Who do you reckon it belongs to?' queried a soldier who had been silent up to that point, looking at the sergeant.

'They do say finders's keepers,' another man pointed out, watching the helpful one boarding the wagon. 'Ain't that right, serge?'

'That's what they say,' declared the non-com.

Although the sergeant could guess at who owned the whiskey – for the Irishmen had not attempted to keep its coming a secret – he refused to make his knowledge public. Like the majority of his regiment, he disliked white men and accompanying the Chicago All-Irish Volunteers had done nothing to make him change his feelings. So he had no intention of returning the consignment to its owners.

Having been granted what they chose to regard as permission, the members of the guard who were not already in possession of bottles swarmed around the wagon. Attracted by their excited shouts, more men hurried up. Hearing the news, they clamoured to be allowed to share in the fortunate arrival.

Standing just inside the fringe of the woodland, Dusty Fog, Billy Jack and the other Texans, except for Kiowa, watched what was happening.

'Looks like they're doing what we want them to,' the lanky sergeant commented, although his tones suggested that the Negroes' behaviour was a tragedy and not a successful part of their arrangements. 'Now some of their officers're sure to come, make 'em put it all back and take it to them Irish jaspers.'

'If they do,' Dusty threatened, 'I'll have something to say at the court martial.'

'What court martial?' Billy Jack inquired.

'The one I'll get you for wishing it to happen,' the small Texan explained, then became more serious. 'Anyways, I'm banking on them all, except the officer-of-the-day, being at the meeting in Searcy.'

'It's possible,' Billy Jack conceded, but contrived to imply that he did not expect it to happen. 'Any time the Commanding General comes a-visiting, every officer busts a gut trying to get to meet him. There's some's calls it "butt-licking".'

'But not you?' Dusty challenged, continuing to watch the camp.

'Me!' the sergeant yelped indignantly. 'Why Mr. Fog, sir, as if *I'd* say such a thing! I'm too loyal—'

'So you keep telling me,' Dusty drawled. 'But I notice that you always seem to know about things like that.'

'Anyways,' Billy Jack said, obviously wanting to change *that* subject. 'The officer-of-the-day'll come and make 'em give it back.'

'Or maybe a swarm of diamondbacks'll come and spook the team, so they bolt across the valley,' Dusty suggested, glancing at his sergeant.

'Knowing *my* luck, it could happen,' Billy Jack warned, wishing that he had thought of such a contingency.

'One thing I know,' Dusty declared, in tones redolent with mock resignation. 'If we get out of this alive, I'm going to find me a more cheerful sergeant.'

'That don't worry me none,' Billy Jack answered. 'With *me* along, we ain't likely to get back alive.'

Watching the Negroes boarding and unloading the

wagon, while others opened the boxes, or distributed the contents, Dusty heard chuckles from his men at Billy Jack's comment. The small Texan grinned. He knew that Billy Jack used the predictions of doom and disaster to help keep up the enlisted men's spirits, or relieve their anxieties in dangerous situations. So he had started to go along with his sergeant, realizing what good morale-boosters such conversations could be. In fact, he admitted to himself, they even helped him in times of stress.

'They're sure getting liquored up,' commented one of the veterans, a touch wistfully.

'I'd sooner we was drinking it than them,' the second old hand went on.

'All we'd've got out of it'd've been sore heads in the morning,' Billy Jack pointed out. 'This way it'll be the Yankees's gets 'em.'

'One thing's for sure,' Dusty drawled. 'Unless their officer-of-the-day arrives real soon, he'll not be able to make them obey him. Most of them'll be too drunk to take orders.'

Dusty had not based his strategy upon ideas of Negroes being naturally drunken, shiftless, or irresponsible. The Hardin, Fog and Blaze clan had never owned slaves, nor had there been any in the surrounding counties. The clan's participation in the War, on the side of the Confederacy, had been caused by a belief in the inalienable right of any State to secede from the Union if its interests and policies should prove incompatible with those of the Federal Government.* So, until he had joined the Texas Light Cavalry in Arkansas, Dusty's contacts with coloured people had been few and, if anything, would have led him to form exactly the opposite opinion regarding their behviour.

What the small Texan had counted on was his growing

* This was the major cause of the War Between The States, although the anti-slavery issue was much enlarged upon and exploited in the North to give the white, working class population – who would have been unlikely to understand the implications of the Secessionist issue – an acceptable reason – that they would be helping to set free the poor, ill-used, down-trodden slaves – for enlisting and fighting against their countrymen.

knowledge of men; particularly men who, while serving as soldiers, found themselves away from their homes and removed from their accepted codes of social conduct.

From the sentry's comments, Dusty had deduced that he was completely biased against Negroes, but, as became a good 'one hundred and *ten* per cent'* American, would have been no less prejudiced against any other racial, or religious group.

However, Dusty had decided that the soldier's comments about the Negroes' lack of discipline and military skill might have some basis of truth. Not because they were Negroes, but through a lack of sound, experienced leadership.

Any regiment, the young lieutenant had been taught, was only as good as its officers made it. The correct kind of training and discipline, carried out by officers who had shown themselves to be capable and to know their work, or who took the right kind of interest in the enlisted men's health and welfare, was what built *esprit de corps* and turned a bunch of civilians into a fighting regiment. The Texas Light Cavalry was commanded by officers who possessed those qualities.

According to the sentry, the Negroes' white officers were 'soft shells' who had come into the Army straight from college; their commissions having been handed to them despite their lack of military abilities, because nobody else could be found to take on the task of training the coloured soldiers. That was possible, Dusty had believed, for he had heard that career officers fought shy of serving in the few volunteer regiments of Negroes that had been formed. So the Union Army's top brass might have been willing to take applicants, regardless of knowledge or aptitude.

With that in mind, Dusty had made his plans and gambled on the general lack of discipline prevalent in many volunteer outfits on both sides. Appointed through political

* The story is that, in the course of an argument with an Irishman, an Italian immigrant stated that he was one hundred per cent American. Not to be outdone, the Irishman replied that he was a one hundred and ten per cent American.

or social influence, far too many of the officers had proved lacking in the ability to control the enlisted men. Dusty had believed that this was the case with the Negroes. He had also decided that similar conditions existed amongst the Chicago All-Irish Volunteers. With the absence of most of the officers, the scheme ought to have a good chance of working.

After the arrival of the horses, Dusty had dispatched Billy Jack and the three veterans to escort Sandy with the wagon. They had orders to make the best possible speed, especially while in the vicinity of the cliff. After their companions' departure, the small Texan and Kiowa had tied up but did not gag the unconscious men. Ensuring that the knots were such that the soldiers could release themselves, after a struggle, the Texans had returned to the rim and awaited developments.

By the time the Irishmen had recovered consciousness, the wagon and riders were out of sight and beyond hearing distance. So were the Yankees' mounts, which had bolted during the excitement of the attack. From the profane and lurid comments overheard by the listening Texans, their bait had been swallowed without reservation. The Irishmen were convinced that they had been attacked by members of the Negro regiment. What was more, the furious men had sworn vengeance and, having escaped from their bonds, had started to walk as fast as they could in the direction of their camp.

Once that had happened, Dusty and Kiowa had collected their horses, which had been left at a suitable distance. Then they had separated. Kiowa was to keep the Irishmen under surveillance, while Dusty had pushed on to rejoin the rest of the detail. On his doing so, they had turned off of the trail, making a detour to avoid the Chicago All-Irish Volunteers' camp, and had crossed the valley without being seen by the occupants of the remount depot. With that accomplished, they had arranged for the driverless wagon to go to the Negroes' quarters.

While all had gone well so far, Dusty knew that complete success was still a long way from being assured. However, the prospects were constantly improving. As yet, no officer had made an appearance to investigate the commotion. The longer the arrival of someone in authority was delayed, the smaller grew his chances of being able to accomplish anything with the men.

Laughter, shouts, singing and other evidences of merriment rolled in an increasing volume from the Negroes' camp. More men, drawn from their tents by the noises, joined the milling group about the wagon. Bottles were continually being opened, sampled and passed from hand to hand.

Turning his attention to the other side of the valley, Dusty used the field glasses that he had been loaned before leaving the regiment. He could see figures gathering to look in the Negroes' direction. Even if the Irishmen could not see the wagon, they would be wondering what was causing all the excitement.

The call of a whip-poor-will, repeated twice, reached Dusty's ears from somewhere to his rear. Billy Jack replied in the same manner and, a few seconds later, Kiowa joined them.

'Those jaspers we caught should just about be at their camp, Mr. Fog,' the dark-faced soldier stated. 'They didn't see anybody on the way and, like you told me, I left 'em when they got close to the camp.'

'Then we ought to be seeing something hap—' Dusty began.

At that moment, from across the valley, came yells of anger. The men who had been watching the Negroes were turning to run into the centre of their camp, while others poured from the tents. Louder and more menacing rose the roaring of voices as the crowd grew in size.

Scanning the opposite side of the half-mile wide valley, Dusty tried to discover exactly what was happening. At that distance, even in the bright moonlight, he could not make out the figures clearly enough to hope to identify any of them. Yet he felt sure that the centre of the attraction must be his victims telling their story. Everything now depended on the reaction of their audience. More particularly, the continuation of the affair hinged upon the type of men who had gained promotion as the regiment's non-commissioned officers.

From what Devlin had told him, Dusty assumed that promotion in the Chicago All-Irish Volunteers – at least as far as the enlisted men were concerned – had been mainly on physical qualifications. Working on the principle that a non-com would need to be able to enforce his orders with his fists – regardless of other, more suitable military qualities – the colonel had selected men capable of doing it. In which case, Dusty was gambling on the non-coms being roughnecks more interested in the recovery of 'the O'Bannion's' gift than the maintenance of discipline. If the sentry had spoken the truth, the only officer in the camp was not the kind who could control the enraged soldiers.

The soldiers were scattering, making for their quarters on the run!

Although the rest of Dusty's party did not have field glasses, they could discern enough to see the latest development. The three older soldiers exchanged glances, while Sandy's face showed his disappointment at what he regarded as a sign that the rest of the plan would not work. Darting a look at Dusty, Billy Jack said nothing. The sergeant knew when *not* to make comments on failure, or gloomy predictions of mishaps.

Then the Irishmen started to reappear and assemble at the top of the slope. Through his glasses, Dusty could see the reason for their departures. Every man was carrying his firearm and had his weapon belt strapped about his waist.

'They're coming!' Sandy ejaculated, watching the mass of men pouring towards the bottom of the valley 'That's 'cause they've seen us bunch and know what we've done,' Billy Jack declared. 'Now they're coming all mean 'n' riled up to catch us.'

Detecting the undertone of relief in the sergeant's doleful voice, Dusty grinned. Billy Jack had been just as concerned as he had by the Irishmen's departure, but now realized why it had happened.

Wondering what the occupants of the remount depot were making of the new disturbance, Dusty turned his field glasses in their direction. Previous checks had shown the sentries and soldiers who would be in charge of the horses were looking towards the rims, trying to discover what all the commotion was about. There was more activity now. The sentries were deserting their posts and converging on the mass of advancing men. The remainder of the guard came from their accommodation and made for the slope. Curiosity was causing the depot's staff to accompany the other enlisted men. Three officers, one wearing a cavalryman's uniform, rushed from a tent.

There were shouted explanations, followed by bellows of rage from the men of the guard. Even the depot's staff joined in the mob, caught up by excitement and a desire to do something, anything, to relieve the boredom of their existence.

Yelling commands, the three officers ran to confront the soldiers. On strode the enlisted men. One of the infantry lieutenants, Dusty could not tell which – although he guessed, correctly, that he was from the Negro regiment – tried to draw a revolver. It was a very bad mistake, with the mood the Irishmen were in. Before the weapon was clear of its holster, several soldiers charged. Rifle butts swung and all of the officers were battered to the ground. Forwards swept the crowd, leaving the trio of motionless figures as the only human occupants of the depot.

Directing his glasses back to the Negroes' camp, Dusty saw that they had not been unaware of what was happening. Probably a number of them had suspected, or been sure, to whom the wagon had been intended to be delivered. However, it having come into their possession – and mindful of its owners' animosity towards them – they were disinclined to hand it over. Especially when the Irishmen were clearly coming in such a hostile manner to try to recover it.

Already many of the Negroes had collected their weapons

and others were hurrying to arm themselves. The sight of them standing at the top of the slope, holding their rifles, was all the inducement required by the Irishmen. Weapons on both sides were raised. Just who fired the first shot was uncertain. It could have come from either group and it was followed almost immediately by a ragged volley. Lead slashed up and down the slope, with men falling dead or wounded as some of it found its way into flesh.

'All right,' Dusty said, as the Irishmen started to take cover half-way up the slope. 'Let's go.'

With the Yankee soldiers engrossed in firing at each other, Dusty and his men made only a short detour before reaching the corrals unobserved. Working fast, they opened the gates and drove out the already disturbed and milling animals. With horses and mules bolting along the bottom of the valley, the Texans set fire to the stacks of fodder. Still without interruption from the fighting soldiers, they collected their own mounts and rode away.

'Did you ever see the beat of it?' demanded one of the veterans. 'We've not only chased off all ole "Cussing" Culver's hosses, we've got his fellers killing each other off for us.'

'That sure was slick figuring, Mr. Fog,' the second veteran went on.

'I can't see them mules going far,' Billy Jack protested. 'The Yankees'll likely get most of 'em back comes morning.'

'They won't get many of the hosses,' the third old hand pointed out. 'Most of 'em'll be headed back home.'

'I don't reckon there'll be any of the hay and grain saved,' Sandy McGraw continued, staring in frank admiration at the small Texan as he rode ahead of the detail. 'Them fellers're too busy shooting each other up to think about putting the fires out.'

'Thought you said his fool notion'd never work, Tom,' the first veteran drawled to the second, lowering his voice in the hope that Dusty would not hear.

'You didn't think it would, either,' protested the doubter.

'I ain't gainsaying it,' admitted the first speaker. 'That's one smart young feller we've got bossing us.'

Listening to the words, Dusty felt a surge of pride and satisfaction. He knew his actions that night would go a long way – once told back at the regiment – towards gaining his acceptance as a leader.

While Dusty did not know it, he had struck an even more important blow for the Confederate cause than merely scattering the remounts and destroying the fodder. He realized that the morale of the two regiments would be adversely affected for a long time to come, but did not visualize the full ramifications.

On learning of the incident, General Culver realized the delicate nature of the situation. There had been no hope of hushing it up and the respective colonels were each equally determined that his regiment should not be blamed. So Culver was compelled, reluctantly, to hold a court of inquiry in an attempt to discover what had occurred. He soon saw that there was no hope of establishing the guilt or innocence of either outfit. However, feelings were still running so high between the Irishmen and the Negroes – for both had lost a number of men – that Culver knew he must take some form of action.

Deciding on what type of measures to take had been fraught with difficulties. All the other white outfits under Culver's command tended to side with the Chicago All-Irish Volunteers and were expressing distrust of the coloured soldiers. There was one snag to Culver taking the obvious step. The Negroes' officers had important connections in the political world. So he realized that they could make a lot of trouble for him if he 'victimized' their regiment by sending it away.

Showing a flair for diplomacy, Culver solved the problem by ordering both regiments to return East; where they could 'recruit and bring themselves up to fighting strength'. While that had, at least, saved everybody's face, Culver was left with a far reduced force when he commenced his offensive and could have used the departed soldiers.

Dusty received considerable acclaim for his actions, on returning to the Texas Light Cavalry, and Kiowa Cotton was promoted to corporal for his work as a scout. During the next weeks, through the Yankees' offensive and until the Battle at Martin's Mill, the small Texan worked under Captain von Hertz's direct command and was given no further opportunity to distinguish himself. However, he had continued to hold the enlisted men's esteem.

That was to become important!

Part Four

THE BATTLE OF MARTIN'S MILL, cont'd.

CHAPTER TEN

ONCE clear of the trees, Sergeant Major Goering halted his horse and watched Company 'C' passing by. Despite his misgivings regarding Mr. Fog's decision to ignore their dead captain's plan for making the attack, he wanted to be sure that the men were adopting the echelon formation as required by the young first lieutenant. Fortunately, it was a drill that the Company had frequently carried out. So the men knew what was expected of them without needing long explanations.

Although the two columns were parallel, the men in them formed a staggered pattern. The first and second men of the right hand file rode with a distance of about three yards between their horses and the leading man of the other column positioned his mount opposite the gap. A similar formation extended along the length of the Company so that, when they turned to face the enemy, every man would have an unrestricted field of fire.

When satisfied that all was in order, the sergeant major galloped after and joined his youthful commanding officer.

Accompanied by Sandy McGraw and the bugler, Dusty Fog rode to the right of the Company's line of march. The small Texan had put aside his thoughts of the past and was concentrating on the work at hand. At his signal, the other two slowed their mounts and allowed the columns to go by.

'Tell the men to leave their revolvers holstered, sergeant major,' Dusty requested, as Goering rode up. 'I don't want any shooting until I give the word.'

'Yo!' responded the sergeant major and raised his voice to relay the order.

Dusty left Goering to attend to such details, giving his attention to other matters. Watching the Lancers urging their mounts to a gallop, the youngster wondered if he should increase his Company's pace. After at moment's thought, he decided against giving the command. He wanted to have the men under complete control, which was never easy once they started to gallop, and for the horses to be as fresh as possible when they were required to charge.

Would he be in time if he held the Company to a trot?

There certainly would not be much in it, but Dusty was gambling that they would.

The Lancers sure looked mighty impressive and menacing. Ahead of the leading wave galloped a major and two lieutenants. Unlike their men, they – and the other officers – were armed with revolvers and sabres. They had each drawn the latter weapon and were waving it while encouraging their followers. The enlisted men carried nine foot long lances, made of Norwegian fir and tipped with diamond-shaped, needle-pointed, steel tips; but had no other weapons.

That last point was one of the factors upon which Dusty was basing his strategy. Another, which he had hoped might happen, was already starting to take place. The Lancers had commenced their advance in a kind of triple echelon formation. Already the lines were growing ragged and the men had started to close together as their speed increased. Unless they opened out again, they would be badly bunched before they reached their objective.

Looking from his point of vantage higher up the slope, Dusty decided that only the captain in command of the rear company appeared to have noticed the danger. The youngster could see him yelling and signalling for his men to spread out, or drop back a short distance and regroup. Apparently the words were falling on deaf ears.

Dusty swung his gaze from the Lancers, to make an examination of the rest of the battleground.

At the mountain battery, Captain Staunce threw a glance towards the Lancers. Then he turned his attention to the four howitzers and left control of the small defensive party to his capable sergeant major. They would be an inconsiderable factor in protecting the little guns, but their presence was good for the crews' morale. The safety of the battery really depended on Company 'C' of the Texas Light Cavalry – and they would be outnumbered by around three to one.

All in all, it was a very dangerous situation. Staunce knew that the success of the Confederate attack depended on his howitzers silencing the Yankees' three Vandenburg Volley Guns. He had complete faith in his men's ability to carry out their duty, unless the Lancers prevented them from doing it. In that event, Staunce hoped he would be killed and not captured. Although he wore the uniform of a Confederate States' artillery captain, he was not a native of that country.

Not long past his twentieth birthday, Douglas St. John Staunce was the son of Britain's leading artillerist. From his father, he had learned the art of handling cannon and the War Between The States had seemed like a good opportunity for him to gain practical experience in the field. Like Staunce, the men of the battery were British. Veterans of the Crimean War, who had been disenchanted with civilian life in England, he had gathered them when a group of cotton manufacturers had financed the battery and offered him command. Trained in the British fashion of discipline backed by fair play and a sense of humour, they had become a crack outfit. Staunce knew that he could depend upon them to do their best, even without the knowledge of their fate if they should be captured.

'Fire!' Staunce barked, when each piece's gunner had reported that it was trained and ready.

Four hands tugged sharply at lanyards, causing friction

primers* to ignite and touch off the powder charges. With almost simultaneous bellows, the howitzers flung their loads into the air. Standing upwind, so as to be clear of the smoke, Staunce watched for the results of the shots. They proved to be good. Two of the shells bracketed the Vandenburg farthest from the battery, killing most of its crew when they exploded. The third and fourth shells landed close enough to the remaining Volley Guns to make the men handling them dive hurriedly for shelter.

'Reload!' Staunce yelled. 'Go to it, lads! Independent rapid fire!'

While the gunners changed the friction primers and connected the lanyards, the number two men sponged out the barrels of the pieces. They used water out of the buckets which had been transported suspended under the carriages and filled on arrival from the men's canteens. The third member of each crew dashed to the battery's two-wheeled caisson, of the type known as the 'prairie ammunition cart'. The lid of its forward chest was open and the sergeant in charge handed out 'fixed'† twelve-pounder rounds to replenish the howitzers.

Allowing his men to carry out their duties, Staunce looked towards the woods. To his relief, he found that Company 'C' was on the move. However, von Hertz was nowhere in sight. Instead young Dusty Fog appeared to be in command. Young, maybe, but Staunce did not doubt that – no matter what had happened to the captain – the cavalrymen were being led in a satisfactory manner.

Staunce did not watch the Texans for long. Satisfied that they were coming to his aid, he devoted his attention to the working of his howitzers.

Allowing half of the men to go by, with Billy Jack controlling their speed at the front and Sergeant 'Stormy' Weather bringing up the rear, Dusty and his party increased their horses' speed to match that of the rest of the Company.

* A description of how a friction primer works is given in: *The Hooded Riders*.

† 'Fixed' round: one with the cartridge bag attached to the shot.

Without waiting for orders, leaving his superior to concentrate on the tactical situation, Goering told the men opposite his party to open up a gap. That would ensure they were able to start shooting once the turn had been made.

Watching the Lancers, Dusty compared their pace to that of his men. He also gauged the distances involved and knew there would be little margin for error.

Thinking only of the relative positions of his Company, the battery and the Lancers, Dusty guided the Texans into the narrowing gap between the former and the latter. He could sense a growing tension among his men and saw that all of them were watching the Lancers. Many, especially the younger, less-experienced soldiers, were fingering the butts of their revolvers. However, so far they were showing no signs of disobeying, or anticipating his orders.

Dusty knew that the situation could easily change. If one of the anxious, or over-eager, riders should turn on the enemy prematurely, others were sure to follow his example. Only with a massed, concerted effort could Company 'C' hope to achieve anything against the Yankees' superior numbers.

Everything hinged upon how much faith the men had in Dusty's judgment.

What to do for the best was not an easy decision for a young officer, freshly thrust into command, to have to make. Especially when the future of the Confederate States' Army of Arkansas and North Texas hung precariously in the balance and his actions could easily tilt the scales in the wrong direction.

The moment had come for Company 'C' to turn and face the enemy!

'Columns right, yo!' Dusty called, reining his bay around until its head was pointing at the horse ridden by the Lancers' commanding officer.

The superb horsemanship of the Texans soon became evident. Rider after rider swung his mount to the right. While they did not make their turns like puppets coupled to a single string, they came around sufficiently in unison to form the solid body that Dusty required for his purposes.

In a few seconds, deftly controlling the restlessness caused to their horses by the mountain battery's howitzers bellowing not too far away, the twin columns that had been passing across the Lancers' front had changed into two staggered lines heading towards the blue-clad soldiers.

'Rear column forward!' Goering reminded in a booming tone, looking back across his shoulder.

Urging their horses to a faster pace, the men at the rear advanced until they filled the gaps in the front line. Without needing orders. Sandy McGraw and the bugler slowed down until they too occupied their positions in the Company. Dusty and Goering continued to stay ahead of the enlisted men, as was their right and duty. It was good for the soldiers' morale to see their superiors in front of them as they rushed to meet an enemy.

With the Company turned towards the Lancers, Dusty prepared to carry out the next part of his plan. Nodding in confirmation to the sergeant major's unasked question, he knotted the split-ended reins to his saddle's horn.

'Secure your reins!' Goering bellowed.

One of the drills carried out regularly at Colonel Blaze's instigation had been much enjoyed by the enlisted men, few of whom had bothered to consider the full perils that would be entailed by doing it in action. It was to make a charge with a weapon in each hand – they could be two revolvers, or a handgun and a sabre – while guiding the horses with knee-pressure instead of using the reins.

That was the means by which Dusty hoped to prevent the Lancers from overrunning Captain Staunce's battery.

While the Texans duplicated Dusty's actions, Goering and the other Germans – who were still using their McClelland saddles and U.S. Army bridles – merely dropped their one-piece reins over the pommels. Then they all awaited the next command, which would be to arm themselves.

It did not come!

Instead, the men of Company 'C' continued to rush with empty hands towards the mass of charging Lancers.

CHAPTER ELEVEN

RIDING alongside Second Lieutenant Charles William Henry Blaze, with the six privates following close behind, Corporal Vern Hassle could sense restlessness and tension in the air. The white-haired old timer guessed that the rest of the detail were disturbed and anxious over the change in leadership. One thought was uppermost in each of the enlisted men's minds. They would rather have been under the command of Mr. Fog while handling such a tricky, dangerous and important assignment.

Although he did not show it, Red Blaze was equally aware of the five soldiers' misgivings. He had noticed them studying him in a somewhat critical manner when he had joined them and had known why. He was popular with the enlisted men, due to his amiable nature, good humour and general disregard for strict military discipline, but he lacked his small cousin's personality and ability to inspire confidence. The detail had expected to be led by Dusty Fog and were dubious about their chances now that Red had taken charge.

As Billy Jack had surmised that day outside Arkadelphia, Red was liked by the men of Company 'C', but he had not come anywhere near to gaining the kind of respect earned by Dusty Fog. There had been too many incidents which, while amusing, were not likely to have increased his prestige as an officer.

Soon after his arrival at the regiment, Red had been told to take half of the Company on skirmishing training. All the men concerned had been veterans, with considerable practical experience in that type of duty. So Red had decided that it would be a waste of time and effort to put them through their paces. Captain von Hertz had found the party lounging at ease in a hollow, which had not enamoured him towards the young red-head.

However, after Dusty had explained that an officer must carry out orders if he expected the enlisted men to do as he told them, Red had never repeated that mistake. From then on, he had performed his duties well enough, but it had taken time for him to recover from the consequences of his misguided leniency. At first, the men had expected it to be continued. Eventually they had realized that when he gave an order, he intended to have it obeyed. Unfortunately, he had had a tendency to show in an unfavourable light on other counts. For one thing, if there was a fight when he was around, he was certain to become involved in it.

Red's willingness to shed his jacket and waive all thoughts of differences in rank if challenged or provoked had earned him a reputation – particularly as he had proved to be very adept in all aspects of rough-house brawling and more than able to hold his own in a fight – but it was not one to foster faith in his ability as a military leader. Rather he was considered as a brave, hot-headed, impulsive, if likeable youngster who occasionally said, or did, rash things on the spur of the moment and frequently regretted them later.

Despite his disappointment at having to miss out on the opportunity to side his Cousin Dusty in what ought to be a memorable fight, Red fully realized the importance of his mission. If he failed, the assault would be of little use. With the bridge over the Ouachita River destroyed, the supply column could not cross and would be trapped by the Yankee Army.

It was the first time since Red had joined the Texas Light Cavalry that he had been trusted with a task involving so much responsibility. The thought of the consequences of failure had a sobering effect upon his normally ebullient spirits. He was grimly determined that he would carry out his duty to the best of his ability.

'What d'you-all reckon's waiting for us, Mr. Blaze?' Hassle asked, having drawn certain conclusions regarding the young officer's fitness for the work ahead and wanting to try to verify them.

'A whole mess of Yankees,' Red replied.

'Any notions on where they're likely to be?' Hassle wanted to know.

'Was it me,' Red answered, I'd have vedettes spread through the woods all the way to the river, but hold the main bunch somewhere close to the middle so they're handy for getting to wherever they're needed.'

'Could be,' drawled the ancient corporal, having made much the same deduction. He was aware that the other men were gathering closer to hear what was being said and continued, 'Do you reckon we'll have enough time to keep hid in these woods, all the way down to them along the river?'

'Nope,' Red admitted. 'So we'll only keep in them until we can cut across behind the Lancers.'

As he spoke, Red surreptitiously studied the reactions of the enlisted men. The privates were all looking at Hassle and Red felt vaguely annoyed by their apparent need to seek the corporal's opinion. Then he remembered that, in the early days, the soldiers had acted in a similar manner when Dusty had made a decision.

It was, Red realized, up to him to prove that he was worthy of command. Only after he had achieved that would the men accept his decisions. He also guessed that, at that moment, how the corporal responded to his suggestion was important. The privates were looking to Hassle for guidance.

'I was hoping's you'd say that, Mr. Blaze,' the non-com declared. 'Likely them jaspers by the river'll not be expecting us to come at 'em from that way.'

Guiding his party along the fringe of the woodland, Red kept them amongst the trees. He watched the Lancers and, when he considered it safe to do so, turned at an angle down the slope. On riding into the open, he experienced a moment of uncertainty and wondered if he had appeared too soon. However, if any of the Lancers saw his detail, they gave no indication of it. Instead of a section being dispatched to intercept the eight Texans, they all continued to rush in the direction of the mountain battery.

With that particular danger having gone by, Red led his men along a line which would allow them to reach the woods fringing the river; but keeping them beyond the range of the rifles held by the foot soldiers in the trenches.

'Just look at them Lancers go,' suggested one of the detail, as they were approaching the trees. 'Anybody'd think they didn't like us Johnny Rebs, way they're taking on.'

'Our boys'll sure take the curl out of their tails,' enthused another. 'Trust Mr. Fog to see to that.'

'Wished I was with the Company,' yet a third declared.

'Now me,' remarked the first speaker, who went by the name of Wilbur and was the youngest of the enlisted men. 'I'd say we was safer away from such dangerous fellers. I'd surely hate to have one of 'em trying to poke me with his sticker.'

'That don't worry me none,' grunted the third speaker. 'They'd have to come close enough to do the sticking first. Which me 'n' my ole Army Colt'd have a whole heap to say about *that.*'

'Talking about Army Colts,' the fourth member of the detail put in. 'If I was with the Company, I'd sure's hell have mine out by now.'

Listening to the men, Red grinned tolerantly and turned his head, meaning to make a remark to Hassle. He discovered that the corporal was staring hard at the trees. Then, as if feeling Red's eyes on him, the old timer swung a cold-eyed glare around. Although the leathery features showed nothing of Hassle's thoughts, the youngster realized that he did not approve of what was going on behind them. For a moment Red was puzzled by the corporal's attitude, then he realized what was causing it.

'You bunch watch where we're headed and forget the Lancers!' Red advised coldly. 'Could be they ignored us because they *know* there's somebody waiting and watching, ready to hand us our needings.'

'Shucks,' Wilbur answered cheerfully. 'They ain't likely to

have anybody watching where the Lancers've just come from.'

'I'm not fixing to count on that,' Red warned. 'I'm a heap too young and lovable to want to get killed.'

'I'm all old, ornery 'n' ugly, but I don't want that neither,' the ancient – yet far from decrepit – corporal went on. 'So I floats my stick 'long of you, Mr. Blaze. It'd be the Yankees' way to do something real sneaky like that.'

Maybe Red's unsupported word would not have carried much weight with the enlisted men, but Hassle's agreement caused them to accept the warning. So they turned their attention to scanning the edge of the woodland in search of enemies.

When selecting men for the assignment, Dusty Fog had made certain to impress them with its full importance. He had also warned them of the possible dangers. All they had needed was for somebody to jolt those facts into their thoughts once more.

Finding that young Red Blaze – none of them thought of him as 'Mr.' – appreciated the dangers had given the men more confidence in him. He had pointed out one of the things his cousin had mentioned, but which they had forgotten. Doubtless the Yankees would have anticipated such an attempt would be made and had taken steps to prevent it. If there should be vedettes watching and more men waiting, the detail's task was anything but a sinecure. The penalty for growing unwary under those conditions could easily be death.

Taking time out from his scrutiny of the woods, Hassle glanced behind him. All the men were now watching their front and disregarding whatever might be happening between the Company and the Lancers. In the corporal's opinion, Mr. Blaze was shaping up as well as he had anticipated. All he needed was just a little hint, to show him when he was starting to go wrong. The way in which he had just responded proved that he was willing to accept advice from an older, more experienced subordinate.

'Fan out,' Red ordered, without needing the corporal to

prompt him, and drew the Spencer carbine from its boot under his left leg. 'And keep your eyes to the front, no matter what goes on behind.'

Following his own instructions, Red searched for signs of danger. When he failed to locate any, he grew uneasy. An old adage of Indian-fighting was that the time to start worrying was when you *didn't* see any of them. So he decided that he had the right to start worrying. Besides, if the Yankees did not have vedettes keeping watch, his men might regard him as an alarmist who spooked for no reason. That would cost him what little esteem he had acquired.

Standing with his back resting against the wide trunk of an oak tree, at the edge of the woodland, Private Blumfeld of the 18th 'Wisconsin' Heavy Infantry looked sleepily into the branches. That he was neglecting his duty did not bother him, for he was very tired after the long, gruelling forced march and the work of preparing defensive positions. On top of that, he felt he was wasting his time. The Lancers had ridden by his position on their way to attack the mountain battery, so he considered it extremely unlikely that any Rebels would come in his direction. To do that, they would have to cross the open country in plain sight of the Lancers and the men in the trenches.

Any attempt to out-flank the regiment's positions or prevent the destruction of the bridge, Blumfeld had repeatedly told himself, would be made by moving through the woods along the edge of the river. He considered that, if he had to be sent on picket duty, he should have been placed where he could do something useful instead of in a position where nothing was likely to happen.

Hearing the sound of hooves, Blumfeld sighed. Some of the Lancers must be returning. Maybe he had better look as if he was carrying out his duty, useless as it might be, in the correct manner. Turning, he started to step from behind the tree.

Looking idly towards the riders, Blumfeld's brain started to record details. Then it screamed a warning that something was very wrong. The horsemen, who he had assumed to be part of his regiment's cavalry screen, wore uniforms of cadet-grey and did not carry lances!

Fright lent speed to Blumfeld's limbs, for it was his first contact with the enemy. Jerking his long Springfield rifle-musket into the firing position, he sighted quickly and squeezed the trigger. To his horror, he realized that he had been seen by the riders. While the recoil's kick was still taking the barrel into the air, he sprang to his left.

'Look out, Mr. Blaze!' exclaimed Corporal Hassle, watching the Yankee emerge from behind the tree.

Even as the old timer ended his warning and swung his Henry rifle towards his shoulder, the Springfield banged. Its heavy calibre ball struck the star-in-a-circle badge, jerking Red's hat from his head. The loss of his hat and a narrow escape from death meant little to the youngster when confronted by such convincing proof that his warning to the men had been justified.

Squinting along the barrel of his repeater and allowing for the up and down motion of his horse, Hassle depressed the Henry's trigger. Flipping down, then up, the loading lever, he ejected the empty case and fed another bullet from the magazine tube to the chamber.

'You missed, Vern!' Wilbur scoffed.

'He jumped back while I was aiming,' the corporal replied. 'That ain't what I calls sport—'

There was a sudden, roaring thunder of army revolver shots. They were followed by the screams of stricken horses, the thuds of numerous heavy bodies crashing to the ground and cries of men in pain.

'Keep watching those blasted trees!' Red bellowed, despite the anxiety he was experiencing over his Cousin Dusty's safety now that the badly outnumbered Company had made contact with the enemy. 'There's sure to be more of them waiting for us.'

A faint grin creased Hassle's seamed, grim old face at the youngster's words. Mr. Blaze had said the right thing, without needing any reminding or prompting. What was more important, the enlisted men were taking heed of his warning.

There were some in Company 'C' who might have been worried, or even out-and-out alarmed, when Captain von Hertz had taken lead. The ancient corporal had not been numbered amongst them. Over the years, he had become a shrewd judge of human nature and had learned to assess character with some accuracy. So he had been willing to bet that Mr. Fog would be able to replace the dead captain and was just as capable of dealing with the Lancers.

Nor had Hassle been perturbed when Mr. Blaze had been put in charge of the detail. The shavetail might not have Mr. Fog's flair for leadership; but Hassle had believed that he would do to ride the river with, even if the water should be high among the willows. So the corporal had been willing to back Mr. Blaze's play and give him a nudge in the right direction if it was needed.

Something thudded into the tree's trunk as Blumfeld returned to his place behind it. For an instant, he was puzzled by the sound. The realization came. That white-haired old bastard had taken a shot at him and, despite being astride a fast-moving horse, had come very close to making a hit.

Panic bit at Blumfeld. A young recruit, he had not previously come under fire and found the sensation most unpleasant. What was more, he had emptied his only weapon – he did not regard his bayonet in that light – at the Texans. Reloading a Springfield was a slow, tedious process, even when one's nerves were not flurried. Even if he reloaded, he could not hope to deal with all eight riders before they reached him. Especially as each of them had been holding a Henry or a Spencer repeater. What was more, he had been given definite orders by Sergeant Lipski. If he saw any hint of enemy activity coming his way, he was to return and warn the picketing force.

Having reached that conclusion in a remarkably short time, and growing conscious of the sound of hooves coming closer, Blumfeld dropped his rifle. He tried to remain concealed by the oak tree as he started to run away.

'There he goes!' whooped one of the detail and raised his Spencer, trying to line it at the fleeing soldier.

'Don't shoot!' Red snapped. 'You're likely to need the bullets before we've finished today.'

'That's for sure,' Hassle agreed, having made no attempt to use his Henry. 'He's only the first of 'em.'

'We'll make jim-dandy targets on these horses, Vern,' Red remarked, when the man refrained from firing.

'Sure will, Mr. Blaze,' Hassle replied.

'I dearly love walking,' Red went on, slowing his big brown gelding. 'But only when I've got a horse under me to do it. All right, boys. We'll go the rest of the way on foot.'

'My ma didn't raise her favourite son to be a puddle-splasher,'* Hassle moaned, secretly delighted that Red had once again reached the right conclusion.

'You'll make a real fine one,' Red assured him and stopped the brown. The other men followed his example and he looked at the nearest of them. 'You see to the horses, Wilbur.'

'Shouldn't we just—' the soldier in question began, not relishing the idea of being given such a menial task.

'I'm not asking you to do it as a *favour*, soldier!' Red barked, modelling his tone and attitude on how he believed his Cousin Dusty would have handled a similar situation. 'I told *you* to hold the horses. Now get the hell down and see to it.'

Instead of obeying immediately, Wilbur looked at the other members of the detail. If he had hoped to see any support for his unfinished suggestion, he was disappointed. His companions were studying him with blank indifference and obviously intended to leave the issue between him and their young officer. There was just a hint of warning in Corporal Hassle's cold-eyed scrutiny, but he neither moved nor spoke.

'Hit the ground, *pronto*!' Red continued in a hard growl, glaring straight at Wilbur. He had seen the other men's reactions and knew he must bend the soldier to his will or lose all control of the detail. 'If I have to tell you again, I'll knock you out of that saddle!'

* Puddle-splasher: derogatory name for an infantryman.

Wilbur suddenly realized that Red meant every word he had said. Grim, deadly determination throbbed in his voice and showed in his normally cheerful, freckled face. Meeting the red-head's glare, Wilbur became fully aware of the change that had come over him. No longer was he the easy-going young shavetail who had frequently been in trouble with von Hertz because of his disregard for military matters. Instead, he looked mean, hard and ornery; much as Mr. Fog did when riled or crossed. What was more, Wilbur knew that Red – Mr. Blaze – was just as capable as his cousin of backing up such a threat.

Maybe Wilbur could not claim to be one of the smartest men in the Texas Light Cavalry, but he figured that he had sense enough to know when the time had come to yell 'calf-rope'* and obey orders without argument.

Watching Wilbur swinging hurriedly from his saddle, Hassle concealed a grin. The corporal had been ready, if not willing or eager, to help Red enforce the order and felt pleased that he had not been called upon to do so. It was better for all concerned that the members of the detail realized they had an officer who could and *would* make his decisions stick.

'Here, Wilbur,' Red said, in a gentler tone, as he dismounted and held out his reins. 'Let us get a head start, then come after us.'

'Yo!' answered the soldier.

'Don't get eager and crowd us too close,' Red went on. 'If you do, you could get shot. Should *that* happen, try to fall on the reins and stop the horses getting away. We'll need 'em when we've done what we came for.'

Listening to the chuckles – in which Wilbur joined – that greeted Red's comment, Hassle scored up another point in the youngster's favour. Red had asserted his authority and was now showing the right kind of attitude. There were grins as the rest of the detail joined him on the ground and handed their reins to Wilbur. Then, at Red's order, they spread out into a skirmishing line that had him and Hassle as

* 'Calf-rope': cowhands' expression for admitting surrender.

its centre. Carrying their repeaters at what bayonet fighters termed the 'high port' position, which would allow the weapons to be brought rapidly into whatever kind of use was required, they started to move into the woodland.

The unwilling horse-holder watched his companions depart, then made ready to carry out his duty. Fastening the reins of Red's gelding to his own mount's saddlehorn, he secured Hassle's to Red's in the same manner and continued until all of the animals were attached in a line.

'All right, blast you,' Wilbur said, returning to his horse and taking hold of its reins. 'Let's go slow and easy. I'd hate like hell to get shot and not fall on the reins, although that'd serve Mr. Blaze right for handing me this no good chore.'

Having delivered that sentiment, the soldier led the horses in the direction taken by his faster-moving, unencumbered companions. He grinned as he watched Red until the trees hid the youngster from sight. There was one tough young cuss and he was nowhere near as easy-going as a lot of folks imagined. Anybody who sold him short when there was a job of work to do stood a better than fair chance of wishing that such a notion had never come.

Glancing first right, then left, Red was satisfied with what he saw. Every enlisted man in the detail had been a member of the Texas Rangers before enlisting in the Army. Experienced in all aspects of fighting Indians, the Rangers' primary occupation before the War, they needed no advice on how to handle the kind of work they were doing.

Keeping roughly in line and close enough for easy communication one with another, they were picking their own routes and darting from cover to cover. As they advanced, they scanned the terrain ahead of them constantly. All had learned the importance of unceasing vigilance when stalking an enemy.

'There goes that blue-belly bastard, Mr. Blaze!' announced the soldier at Red's left, gesturing ahead with his Spencer carbine. 'I'll drop hi—'

'Leave him be, all of you!' Red commanded, watching the Yankee infantryman come briefly into view running as fast as his legs would carry him. 'There's no sense in letting his *amigos* know for sure which way we're coming.'

'Was just thinking that meself,' commented Hassle, from Red's right.

Lowering his weapon without firing, the soldier resumed his advance. The infantryman continued to run ahead of the detail. They could only see him at infrequent intervals, obtaining brief glimpses through the gaps in the bushes or between the trunks of the trees.

'Have you seen any of them yet, Vern?' Red inquired, after they had covered about a hundred yards.

'Nary a sign,' the corporal admitted, interrupting his scrutiny for a moment. 'But they're around somewheres. I feel it in me bones. Just wish I could see some of 'em. I hates surprises.'

'Trouble with you is you wants things too easy,' Red scoffed, but did not permit the levity to prevent him examining what lay ahead. 'That's the worst of fighting Indians. They don't make things hard enough, way they come a-whooping and a-hollering. So you – *Look*!'

The final exclamation burst from Red's lips as the fleeing soldier made one of his sporadic appearances. Skidding to a halt, he peered up at the foliage of a flowering dogwood tree and pointed excitedly to his rear.

'Reb's!' the soldier screeched, to all intents and purposes addressing the leaves and branches. 'They're coming, Sergeant Lipski! They're coming and'll soon be here.'

CHAPTER TWELVE

'Weapons, sir?' Sergeant Major Goering prompted, wondering why his young superior had not given the expected order.

Keeping his eyes fixed on the approaching Lancers, Dusty Fog thought fast before replying. If he gave permission for his men to arm themselves, he ran the risk of somebody starting to shoot long before it was advisable to open fire.

What Dusty wanted – in fact, the only thing that would serve his purpose was a volley from every member of the Company. A straggle of individual shots might inflict a few casualties, but would do nothing to halt the Lancers.

On the other hand, Dusty wanted to have his men holding their weapons before giving the order to increase speed.

There was something else for the small Texan to consider. The sight of Company 'C's' drawn weapons – especially the revolvers which every man carried – might have an unnerving effect upon the Lancers. Some, at least, would realize the inadequacy of a lance when opposed by a man with a firearm.

There was, Dusty decided, only one answer.

'Yes, sergeant major,' he said. 'But no shooting until I give the word.'

'Draw pistols and sabres!' Goering commanded in his stentorian tones. 'Hold your fire until ordered.'

Having given his consent, Dusty carried out the process of arming himself. His right hand reached for and slid the sabre from its sheath. Designed to meet his physical requirements, by the Haiman Brothers' best craftsmen and from their finest steel, the blade was two inches shorter and somewhat lighter than one of the standard issue. Dusty did not consider that to be a disadvantage. Due to his size, he found the regulation weapon cumbersome. While he could handle one adequately, if circumstances compelled him to do so,* he achieved better results with the sabre that had been made especially for him.

Crossing his body, Dusty's left hand opened the flap of the holster and he drew out the bone-handled Colt 1860 Army revolver. It belonged to a pair that had been a present from his father. He only carried the one – and used the awkward, unsatisfactory close-topped military holster – because Captain von Hertz had never approved of him wearing the more practical Western-style gunbelt with which he was already something of an expert.

Seeing that the Texans were arming themselves, the trio of officers ahead of the Lancers started shooting. As about two hundred and fifty yards separated the two parties, Dusty wondered if they were doing it for a deliberate reason. Firing from the backs of galloping horses at that range, they could hardly hope to score hits.

Maybe they had guessed Dusty's purpose and were hoping to provoke his men into a premature retaliation!

'Hold your fire!' Dusty bellowed, an instant before Goering could give a similar command. 'Don't let anybody start shooting, you sergeants!'

'That goes for you, you hame-headed yahoo!' Sergeant Weather bawled, glaring along the line at a soldier who was elevating his Colt. 'Wait for the order, god-damn it!'

Looking sheepish, the man in question lowered his weapon. It did not pay to disregard Mr. Fog's wishes, especially when Stormy Weather was helping to enforce them.

'Don't none of you go riling them Yankees by shooting at 'em!' bleated Sergeant Billy Jack at the other end of the line. 'They'll get mean if you do and I could get hurt.' His voice hardened. 'That means you-all, Jones!'

Maybe the lanky non-com's miserable, hangdog attitude

* This is proven in the 'A Convention Of War' episode of: *Under the Stars and Bars*.

might have led a stranger to forming the wrong conclusions about his character, but the man he had named was fully aware of his true potential. So Jones' obedience, and the fact that the others who heard took heed of the warning, did not stem from concern over annoying the enemy.

'At the gallop,' Goering ordered, watching and interpreting Dusty's signal correctly. 'Yo!'

Throwing a quick glance at the hamlet, as he and his men built up their mounts' gaits to a manoeuvring gallop, Dusty saw that the howitzers were continuing with their work. The central Vandenburg's carriage had a broken wheel and its muzzle pointed into the air, rendering it useless. However, the other two Volley Guns would be operable once their crews rose from having dived into cover to avoid the mountain battery's shells.

More shots were coming from the major and two lieutenants, drawing Dusty's attention back to them. Still none of their bullets had taken effect as far as he could tell. Nor had any of his men thrown off the bonds of discipline and replied in kind. Yet they were certain to be resenting being fired upon and doing nothing in return.

'Let them waste their lead, men!' Goering advised, having realized the value of the opening volley. 'Our turn will come.'

The two sergeants were also aware of what their youthful officer was hoping to achieve. So they lent their advice to Goering's and added suitable threats against anybody who failed to obey.

One hundred yards separated the converging bodies of men.

Seventy-five yards!

Fifty.

Dusty set his teeth grimly. To hold on was inviting casualties among his men and the chance that some of them would open fire before he gave the command. If only one man cut loose, others were sure to follow his example and all hope of a devastating close-range volley would be lost.

Another ten yards was diminished from the distance between the Texans and the Lancers.

The Yankee major was taking careful aim!

Flame spurted from the revolver in the major's hand. Giving a croaking cry, Goering jerked spasmodically and slid sideways from his saddle.

Like the sharpshooter earlier, the major had made the error of misjudging Dusty's potential. Believing that the burly sergeant major was responsible for Company 'C's' well-managed manoeuvring, the Lancers' commanding officer had decided that his removal would throw the Rebels into confusion.

'Hold your fire!' Dusty shouted; hating to have to give the order which delayed avenging Goering, but accepting that it must be done and that he would be more than repaid by the volley.

The Lancers had lowered their weapons into the attacking position. Steel points, looking as sharp as needles, extended before the horses in an awe-inspiring manner. They looked mighty dangerous and menacing. Especially to men who were riding with their reins lashed to the saddlehorns, guiding the horses by knee-pressure – which did not permit a great deal of fancy evasive action to be taken.

Studying the sight, Dusty could guess at the tensions rising amongst the enlisted men. If they had had less faith in him, they would have disregarded the order and started shooting.

'Take aim!' Dusty called, thrusting forward his Colt.

Before aligning his sights, the small Texan glanced left and then right. On either side, his men were pointing their revolvers in the Lancers' direction. It would, he guessed, be an impressive – maybe even frightening – sight. More than one member of the Yankees' leading company must be all too aware that he was far beyond a distance at which the weapon he held would be of any use.

'Ready!' Dusty continued, returning his gaze to the Colt's barrel. He pointed it straight at the centre of the major's chest, ignoring the flame which erupted from his target's gun-filled fist and the eerie sound of a bullet winging close by his head. 'Fire!'

Giving the word that his men had been awaiting, Dusty squeezed the Colt's trigger and the hammer pivoted forward. Propelled by the explosive force of thirty grains of powder, the .44 conical bullet spun through the rifling grooves. It belched out of the muzzle and flew unerringly to its objective.

Jolting under the impact, the major threw aside his weapons and clutched at the wound. Feeling its rider swaying, the horse swerved to the right and pitched him off its back.

Following immediately on the heels of Dusty's shot, some sixty revolvers of various types and calibres spewed out their loads in a thunderous, rolling cacophony.

From the results he saw, Dusty concluded that the majority of the Company had taken the trouble to aim before discharging their weapons. Both the lieutenants were hit and toppled from their mounts. At least ten horses were falling, flinging their riders from them. Still others had been less seriously hurt, but started rearing and plunging in pain. Possibly a dozen of the enlisted men had taken lead. In fact, the whole of the Lancers' leading rank appeared to be in some way affected by the Texans' volley.

It soon became apparent that Dusty's strategy had been correct and he was justified in his insistence that the men did not open fire until they had come to close quarters.

Having gathered together, for mutual protection and to present as imposing a front as possible to their enemies, the Lancers were ideally positioned to suffer the fullest impact of the Texans' gun-play. Although only the foremost company had taken the punishment, those who followed were thrown into confusion.

If the second and third companies had kept their distances, they could have averted much of what was coming. Instead, the excitement of the charge and a general lack of control being exercised by their officers had induced them to crowd almost to the rumps of the horses ahead of them. Even the captain commanding the rear company had failed to restrain his men.

As a result of the Lancers' undisciplined folly, a state of pandemonium resulted from the arrival of the Texans' volley. Many of the riders in the centre rank tried to swerve away, to halt even, so as to avoid trampling upon fallen companions. Others were unable to control their mounts and crashed over horses which lay on the ground. The men of the rearmost rank found themselves in much the same position.

Company 'C' had dealt the Lancers a terrible blow and their youthful commanding officer had every intention of following up their advantage. Dusty realized that he dare not allow considerations of humanity to weaken his determination. If he hesitated, their enemies would recover from the shock, regroup and continue the attack on the battery.

'Pour it into them, boys!' Dusty exhorted at the top of his voice, cocking the Colt aided by the kick of its recoil and sending its next load through the head of a survivor in the front rank.

There was no real necessity for the order. Once the enlisted men had been allowed to start shooting, they continued to do so. More lead slashed its way into the disorganized Lancers, clearing saddles in the second and third ranks. Before any of the Yankees could recover from the devastating effect of the first volley, or attain any form of cohesion, the men of the Texas Light Cavalry closed in upon them like wolves attacking a cornered herd of pronghorn antelope.

With his bay hurdling the major's body, Dusty saw a lance being thrust in his direction from the right. He responded automatically. Using the flat of the blade, so that it would not cut into and be trapped by the wood, he deflected the Norwegian fir shaft outwards. With the attack parried, he disengaged the sabre. Turning his hand so that the palm was uppermost, he lunged and sank the point deep into his assailant's chest. Confronted by the onrushing bay gelding, the Lancer's horse tried to swerve. Dusty's mount rammed the other animal with its shoulder and knocked it staggering with a force that tore the sabre from the small Texan's hand.

As the stricken soldier carried Dusty's sabre away from him, he found that another lance's head seemed to be hurtling in his direction. It was coming from the left, wielded by a wild-eyed, yelling corporal, and aimed so that it would catch the young officer in the stomach.

Although Dusty had been deprived of one weapon, he held another equally effective in his left hand. At that moment, the ambidextrous powers he had developed early in his young life – as a means of distracting attention from his small size – came in very useful. Almost as if drawn by a magnet, the Colt in his left hand turned and flame blossomed ahead of its muzzle. He had aimed instinctively and fired the only way he dared under the circumstances; at the head, in the hope of an instantaneous kill.

Back snapped the corporal's head, with blood oozing from where the left eye had been and the base of the skull shattering as the lead emerged. As the man's torso bowed to the rear, the lance's point rose slightly.

Not enough, however!

It was now directed towards the top of Dusty's chest!

What was more, the man's hand had tightened in a death grip on the shaft.

The on-rushing weapon was just as deadly as ever.

CHAPTER THIRTEEN

'GET the hell out of here, you stupid son-of-a-bitch!'

Glowering furiously through the thick foliage of the flowering dogwood tree, into which he had climbed so that he could keep an eye upon the bulk of his picket and obtain a clearer view of the surrounding woodland from above the tops of the numerous bushes, Sergeant Lipski spat out the words as if they were burning his mouth. He had taken a lot of trouble to position and conceal his men, being aware of the importance of their task, and had no desire to see all his work ruined because of Private Blumfeld's panic-induced stupidity.

When Lipski had been ordered to establish a line of lookouts, extending across the woodland to the Ouachita River and protecting the flank of the defences, he had selected his men carefully. Blumfeld should not have been with them. On reaching the dogwood tree and starting to organize his detail, the sergeant had discovered that one of his men had persuaded the inexperienced recruit to take his place.

Instead of telling Blumfeld to return, Lipski had sent him to watch from the edge of the wood. The recruit would be so close to the Lancers that there should have been no danger of him coming into contact with the enemy.

Instead of being safely out of the way, Blumfeld had come dashing back without his rifle and looking scared out of his wits. Unfortunately, he was not so frightened that he had forgotten where Lipski had told the detail he would take up his position. So he had come straight to the tree and started yelling his warning.

'But the Rebs—!' Blumfeld began, indignant at his superior's response to such important news.

'Why the hell don't you go hold their hands and fetch 'em to see where I'm at?' Lipski snarled, scanning the land behind the soldier without locating any sign of pursuit. However, he decided that Blumfeld would not have been mistaken or lying, so went on, 'Head for the bridge and warn Mr. Rosenbaum that they're coming our way.'

After Blumfeld had departed to deliver the message, Lipski glanced around and then stared once more in the direction from which the recruit had come.

The sergeant could not see what was happening beyond the trees, but his ears and knowledge of the general tactical situation enabled him to form fairly accurate conclusions. If the sound of rifles firing volleys was any indication, the Rebels' main assault was well under way. He knew that the Lancers had ridden out earlier than would have been necessary to help disrupt the attackers. That meant they had gone to silence an artillery battery brought up by the Rebs to deal with the Vandenburg Volley Guns.

From a different direction to the rifles had come the crashing of many revolvers and other noises suggesting that the Lancers had met with very stiff opposition. Going by the way that several light cannons – probably mountain howitzers, the sergeant guessed – bellowed repeatedly, although the Vandenburgs did not commence their bombardment, Lipski realized that the Lancers had either failed or been delayed in completing their duty. Maybe the massive multi-barrelled weapons had been put out of action by the shelling.

If that was the case, Lipski figured the situation was growing desperate.

Without the support of the half-battery of Vandenburgs, the 'Wisconsins' would be hard put to hold the bridge. Fortunately, Colonel Middleton had taken that possibility into consideration. Lipski remembered the colonel's orders in the event of their position becoming untenable. Instead of attempting to hold on, they were to withdraw across the river, destroy the bridge and make a long circle to rejoin their advancing army. That ought not to be too difficult, as the

Rebs would be fully occupied in trying to protect their supplies.

There was movement amongst the bushes!

Staring harder, Lipski saw a bare-headed Rebel shavetail and a short, white-haired corporal who looked as old as sin but a whole heap more spry. Other grey-uniformed fly-slicers formed a skirmishing line on either side of the pair. Not many, however. Less than ten, Lipski counted. Which meant his picket had the advantage of numbers.

If only Blumfeld had not betrayed Lipski's position, all would have been perfect.

Yet, although they were advancing carefully, the Rebels did not appear to be aware of the flowering dogwood's significance. Possibly they had not seen Blumfeld's indiscretion, even if they had heard him yelling the warning. They would know that Yankees were about, but would not have any idea of where to look.

Easing back the hammer of his Spencer rifle, Lipski raised the butt to his shoulder. There was an oak tree thirty yards in front of him. By the time the Rebs reached it, they would be within a distance at which the pickets were unlikely to miss them. Commanded by that bald-faced young officer and a decrepit old corporal, the skirmishers ought to be easy meat. Even if they should avoid being shot down in the opening attack, Lipski had another item in his favour. The Texans – their hat-badges told him to which State they belonged – had a habit of calling orders and instructions in Mexican. If they should do so on this occasion, they would betray their purpose. Lipski's corporal spoke Spanish and would be able to translate anything the Rebels said.

At Red Blaze's word, *'Look!'*, the rest of the detail had taken cover before attempting to do so. They listened to Blumfeld giving his warning and exchanged glances.

'That jasper must be kin to my wife,' Corporal Hassle commented dryly, wondering what the man in the tree was thinking about the soldier's indiscreet behaviour. 'They do say stupidity runs in families. It must be *galloping* in his'n.'

'Now me,' Red answered. 'I'm right pleased I didn't let you blood-thirsty yahooes kill him.'

'He's sure obliging, for a Yankee,' Hassle admitted and watched Blumfeld resume his flight. 'What now, Mr. Blaze?'

'We'll keep moving, what else,' Red replied. 'Go extra careful from here on, boys. But don't let on we figure there's a feller in that dogwood. Vern and I'll attend to his needings. You watch out for his *amigos*.'

Continuing their advance the Texans displayed an even greater caution. They studied every bush and tree, with the exception of the dogwood in which the Yankee sergeant was hiding, searching for traces that it might conceal an enemy. Self-preservation demanded that they tried to locate the Yankee pickets before they were exposed to the others' weapons.

Although Red failed to detect any suggestion of danger, he heard Hassle let out low grunts of satisfaction on three occasions and surmised that the corporal had been more successful. He hoped that the remainder of his party were duplicating the old timer's efforts.

Nothing happened as the Texans continued to move forward. The woods about them remained silent, except for the noises of their darting passage from one piece of shelter to the next. Not a shot was fired in their direction and nothing suggested that men might be lurking in concealment, waiting to kill them.

Scuttling to a massive old oak tree about thirty yards from the dogwood, Hassle halted with its trunk between himself and the possible source of danger. Red came to a stop alongside the old timer.

'There's some of them ahead, Mr. Blaze!' called a soldier on the left flank of the line, speaking in Spanish. 'Watch out!'

'Same this side,' continued the man at the extreme right, also using Mexican to avoid giving information to the enemy.

'They've seen some of our boys, serge!' the Spanish-speaking corporal warned, in tones which he hoped would not carry beyond Lipski's hearing.

'Somebody out there knows Mex!' the keen-eared Corporal Hassle said.

'Sounds that way,' Red agreed. 'What do you reckon, Vern. Was that Yankee playing tricky and only pretending there's somebody in that tree?'

'Nope,' the old timer replied. 'I catched just a leetle glimpse of the blue-belly son-of-a-bitch. He's squatting up there like a bluebird on its nest, only not so pretty.'

'And he's not the only one of 'em,' Red drawled.

'There's a fair slew of 'em ahead of us,' Hassle confirmed. 'Four I know about for certain and I've got suspicions on another three. Which ain't counting them's the boys say they've seen.'

'And the ones who've been smart enough to stay hid,' Red said quietly.

'Them too,' Hassle conceded. 'And I'm certain sure some of 'em's slick enough to have kept hid. It's them's'll cause us most grief.'

Red did not need reminding that to move forward without having located the majority – if not all – of the pickets would be inviting disaster. He also knew that he and his men could not stay put and play a waiting game, hoping the Yankees might run out of patience and reveal their positions.

'Let's stir things up a mite,' the youngster suggested and explained what he wanted to do.

'We'd best let the boys know for sure what you're planning, Mr. Blaze,' Hassle replied. 'Which ain't going to be easy, without letting the Yankees know at the same time. One of the sneaky bastards talks Mex.'

'He does,' Red agreed. 'I reckon you speak Comanch', Vern?'

'Some.'

'How about the rest of the boys?'

'They all hail from my neck of the *Nemenuh** country and've had dealings with the red varmints. Likely they'll speak about's much's me, only maybe not so good.'

* Nemenuh: 'The People', the Comanches' name for their nation.

'Good enough for them to understand what I want done?' Red wanted to know.

'I reckon I can get it through to 'em,' Hassle decided. 'Only could be that Yankee talks Comanch' as well as Mex.'

'You're getting to sound like Billy Jack,' Red warned. 'Way I see it, I reckon it's Spanish more than Mex he speaks. So he won't know Comanch'. We'll have to take that chance.'

Raising his voice, Hassle used the dialect of the *Tanima* – Liver Eaters – band to ascertain that the other enlisted men could understand him. Receiving their assurances that they could, he outlined Red's wishes.

'What's that, Garcia?' Sergeant Lipski called, as the old timer's voice reached him.

'I don't know,' the man in question admitted. 'It's not Spanish.'

'Stop that bellowing, damn you!' Red yelled, trying to sound impatient and annoyed. 'Let's go, there's none of the blue-bellied bastards around here.'

'I ain't sure on that, Mr. Blaze,' Hassle protested. 'The boys allow—'

'You heard me!' Red interrupted. 'There's none of them closer than the bridge. The Lancers were covering this part, with the feller we run off in case anybody came after they'd pulled out. Come on, time's a-wasting.'

With that, Red strode around the trunk of the tree. He went with an apparently reckless disregard for possible danger. For all that, he was as alert as an old buck whitetail deer which had been hunted regularly. If he had looked, he would have seen his men emerging from their places of concealment, but with the wary caution arising from greater wisdom and experience. Or so it appeared to the watching Yankees.

Cradling the Spencer's butt to his shoulder, Lipski watched the Texans moving into view. He was not surprised to see the enlisted men displaying more care than the young officer. So far as he could tell, however, they did not realize how close they were to the main body of his pickets.

Certainly the shavetail did not suspect the danger. Just as Lipski had figured, he was a hot-head. It was unlikely that such a man would pose any serious threat to the destruction of the bridge. In fact, the sergeant intended to make sure that he did not.

With the rifle's barrel turning in Red's direction, Lipski remembered the ancient corporal.

The old timer had not yet made his appearance!

That realization came just a moment too late for Lipski.

Instead of leaving the shelter of the oak tree, Hassle had peered around its trunk. From his position, he had been able to make out sufficient of the Yankee sergeant to be aware of what was happening.

'Back!' Hassle snapped, as the Spencer rifle's barrel started to move.

Instantly Red propelled himself swiftly to the rear and sideways. Nor was he a moment too soon. He heard a sharp bang from amongst the dogwood's foliage and, as a bullet ploughed home, a spurt of splinters erupted from the oak's bark about level with his head.

Stepping from his hiding place, with the Henry already lifting to his shoulder, Hassle sighted and fired in what appeared to be a single flowing motion. There was a violent flurry of movement which set the dogwood tree's leaves shaking. Then a Spencer rifle tumbled out, followed by the spasmodically jerking body of the Union infantry sergeant.

Like Red, Hassle did not linger in the open. Having fired and made his hit, he sprang rapidly for the safety offered by the sturdy trunk of the old oak tree. Two bullets hammered into it, instead of finding their billets in his body.

Many more shots sounded as the Texans and the rest of the pickets opened fire at each other. One of Red's men spun around, hit in the head and dead on his feet. Having exposed himself while he was aiming at a Yankee infantryman, he had been killed by another whose presence he had failed to detect.

With lead whistling around them from numerous places,

the Texans were driven back into hiding. It was obvious that the Yankees had set out a strong picket force.

'There's close to twenty of 'em,' Hassle computed, looking at Red. 'And more'n half of 'em's got Spencers. I'd say we're pinned down, Mr. Blaze.'

'Just like Cousin Dusty figured we might be,' Red replied. 'They got Ted.'

'He was unlucky, no more,' the corporal drawled. 'It wasn't your fault. All the boys knowed what you wanted 'em to do and that it wouldn't be easy. You took the biggest chance of all.'

'I've still got to get to the bridge,' Red declared, hiding the relief he was experiencing at Hassle's words. He had been blaming himself for the soldier getting killed. 'The woods on the other side're more open than these. So Company 'A'll' be in an even worse tight than us. So I'm open for suggestions, smart or otherwise, was they to be offered.'

'We could try rushing 'em, horns a-hooking,' Hassle said dubiously. 'Some of us'll get killed for sure, but *maybe* the others'll get through.'

'We daren't go betting on a "maybe", Vern,' Red pointed out.

'One man, moving fast and sneaky, might get down to the river, happen the rest of us keep the Yankees busy.'

'It's possible,' Red drawled.

'You fixing to call for a volunteer, Mr. Blaze?' the corporal inquired hopefully, although his summation of the youngster's character had already told him what the answer would be.

'I've already done it,' Red announced with a grin. 'And, like a dad-blasted fool, it was me who said "I'll go".'

'Try saving some of that lead!' Hassle bellowed, as the other members of the detail exchanged shots with the Yankees. Then he looked at Red and went on, 'That's the way it should be, Mr. Blaze. Are you going to handle it the way Mr. Fog was fixing to?'

'If it was good enough for Cousin Dusty, it's good enough for me.'

'You'll have to slip by any more of 'em's been staked out between here and the river.'

'Sure, unless I can get around them.'

'There's that,' Hassle conceded, ' 'cepting you don't have time to go too far around.'

'So I'll not go *too* far, but move faster,' Red answered.

'Are you going on foot, or as the Good Lord intended when he made us miserable sinners smart enough to catch 'n' tame hosses?'

'Like I said,' Red replied, looking around and thinking fast. 'I dearly hate walking, unless there's a horse under me doing it. And that goes double for *running*.'

'Running'll be a right good way for you to go,' Hassle admitted. 'Except I don't reckon them Yankees'll be too pleasured, happen they see you lighting out.'

'I'm not counting on letting them see me go,' Red declared. 'Tell the boys to cover me.'

While the corporal gave the necessary orders in Comanche, Red leaned his Spencer against the trunk of the tree. Removing his weapon belt, the youngster took the Colt from its holster.

'I don't want anything slowing me down,' Red told Hassle, placing the belt on the ground. 'Start cutting loose and make them think we're fixing to rush them.'

Throwing back his head, Hassle let out the kind of war-whoop used when the *Tanima* Comanche rode to attack the hated white brother. Then he thrust the Henry around the side of the tree. Sighting in the direction of one of the pickets, he threw three shots as fast as he could work the rifle's lever. The remainder of the detail, who had stopped shooting, resumed their bombardment. Instantly every picket in the vicinity, suspecting that this was the prelude of an attack, replied with hot lead.

Red waited until the exchange of fire had built up. Hoping that the attention of the Yankees was set on his men, he sank to his stomach. Hassle stepped over him, swapping the Henry for his Spencer carbine and using it from the other side of the trunk. Knowing what the corporal was trying to do, Red wriggled rapidly across the open land that separated him from a clump of bushes. At every writhing movement, he expected to feel a bullet crashing into his body, or close by, warning that his departure had been observed. It did not happen and, reaching the bushes, he rose cautiously. Hassle's ruse had worked. Being fired on with different weapons from either side of the oak, the Yankees did not know that Red had slipped away.

Keeping in concealment if possible, or running swiftly across such open spaces as came his way, Red darted rapidly through the trees. He had covered about three hundred yards when he saw Wilbur and the horses. The enlisted man was behaving sensibly, Red decided. Having heard the shooting, he had halted instead of leading the animals to where they might be seen by the Yankees.

'Turn my horse loose, Wilbur!' Red called, as he approached the soldier.

'Yo!' Wilbur replied.

To give the soldier credit, he did not for a moment think that Red was deserting their companions. Instead, he realized that the young officer was carrying out the most important part of the assignment.

Releasing his hold on his horse's bridle, the soldier sprang to set free Red's gelding. Before the youngster arrived, Wilbur had also removed Hassle's reins from the brown's saddlehorn. Running up, Red grasped the saddlehorn in his left hand and vaulted on to his mount's back. He was about to ride away when he noticed how Wilbur was staring towards the shooting. There was an almost pleading expression on the soldier's face as he swung his gaze towards his officer.

'All right,' Red said with a grin. 'Fasten up those fool critters and go help the boys.'

'*Gracias*, Mr. Blaze!' Wilbur whooped delightedly. 'Good luck.'

'Likely I'll need it,' Red answered, starting his horse moving and turning it to the south. 'You go careful. There may be more of 'em around.'

Encouraging his gelding to a fast trot, Red listened to the continuing sounds of conflict. Clearly his detail was still contriving to hold the attention of the Yankee pickets. Beyond the woods, going by the noise, the fighting was carrying on with unabated fury at the hamlet and where Company 'C' was locking horns with the Lancers.

Despite all the activity elsewhere, Red's passage through the woods proved to be uneventful. Apparently he had been fortunate enough to have selected a route which was taking him clear of any vedettes set out by the Yankee sergeant. Or they had quit their posts and moved in to help the main body of the picket. Whatever the reason, he came into sight of the Ouachita River without finding use for the Colt in his right hand.

The river lay at the foot of a fairly steep slope. Having seen nothing to disturb him, Red started to make the descent.

Raising a Spencer rifle to his shoulder, a Union Army infantryman sprang from behind a bush ahead of Red. The man was so close that he seemed unlikely to miss.

CHAPTER FOURTEEN

WITH the lance's point passing the head of his bay gelding, Dusty Fog tightened his legs' grip on the saddle and inclined his body to the right. He had to tilt himself farther than he had expected. Even then, he barely escaped being impaled. The lance's diamond-shaped head brushed his left shoulder in passing, but it did him no harm and the corporal's horse carried its lifeless burden by his mount.

Dusty found that he was still in danger. Looming up on his right, a lieutenant belonging to the Lancers' second company was turning a revolver towards him. Hanging by his legs alone, almost beyond the point of balance, Dusty was in no position to protect himself.

Wild with excitement and elation at the success of their volley, the men of Company 'C' gave no thought to being outnumbered. Already they had whittled down the odds against them and felt that victory was assured. So they charged recklessly into the fray. If it came to a point, few of them would have been able to halt, or even divert, their fast-running horses.

'Yeah! Texas Light!'

Uttering their war-yell, the Texans rushed into the Lancers' ranks. Collisions were unavoidable, but the men of Company 'C' were the better riders and came out of the impacts more successfully than their opponents. They had another advantage, being armed with weapons that could be wielded at close quarters.

Sabres swung in glistening arcs, until their blades were reddened with blood. Revolvers thundered and flung death indiscriminately at man or beast. Lances drove into flesh, or were parried to leave their wielders exposed to the would-be victims' counter-measures. Men yelled, cursed, or shrieked in pain. Struck by steel, or flying lead, horses screamed, snorted, reared high, plunged, or collapsed kicking wildly.

To the right and slightly behind Dusty, Sandy McGraw was carrying out his duty by sticking close to his commanding officer. Seeing the small Texan's predicament, the guidon carrier acted fast. Swinging up the Colt in his right hand, he thumbed off two shots as fast as he could squeeze the trigger and work the hammer. He hoped to hit the Yankee officer. Instead, the first bullet missed. The second struck the neck of the lieutenant's horse. Down went the animal, front legs buckling under it, to hurl its rider from its back. Losing his revolver, the lieutenant rolled under and was trampled by Dusty's big gelding.

Even as Sandy intervened, Dusty was grabbing for the saddlehorn with his right hand. Taking hold, he pulled and regained a more secure, upright seat on the gelding's back. A Lancer was passing on Dusty's left. Seeming to move of its own volition, the bone-handled Colt pointed and hurled a bullet into the soldier's ribs as he went by.

Then Dusty found that there was nobody in front or on either side of him. For a moment he was puzzled. Realization flooded over him. He was clear of the Lancer's shattered ranks, having cut and shot his way through them.

Looking behind him, Dusty discovered that the main force of the attack had been halted. Some of the Lancers, who had been on the ends of the ranks had avoided the confusion and continued to charge towards the battery. They were few in numbers and Sergeant Major Smalley's defending force appeared to be dealing with them in a satisfactory manner. Certainly they were not impeding the four howitzers' rate of fire.

The battery was operating independent fire now, with each diminished crew doing its best to attain the greatest speed in reloading and retraining its piece. Following the crash of the Number Four howitzer, there was a much louder than usual detonation at the hamlet.

Curving downwards, the piece's twelve-pound shell plunged into the open chest at the front end of the Vandenburg Volley Guns' solitary ammunition caisson. Ignited by the flash of the howitzer's powder charge going off, the fuse had been burning steadily during the flight. The minute spurt of flame reached the shell's half-pound burster charge at precisely – if luckily – the right moment.

Although the caisson's crew must have realized their peril, they were unable to escape. The shell exploded before any of them could attempt to spring away from the danger area. So did the mass of paper cartridges into which the missile had descended, to be followed in rapid succession by the contents of the second and third chests.

In one blinding instant of roaring sound, the whole of the three multi-barrelled weapons' ammunition supply disintegrated. Along with it went the crew of the caisson, blown into oblivion.

Several of the Texans, including Sandy McGraw and the bugler had also fought their way through the Lancers' disrupted formation. However, the majority were still battling in a wild, savage, no-quarter-asked-or-given melee. Dusty knew that he must return and support his men.

Hooking the fingers of his right hand under the off-side rein, the small Texan ignored the explosion of the caisson. He was more concerned with regaining control of his mount. Having accomplished that, he started to guide it in a half circle so that he could get back into the fight.

Riding towards the mass of struggling figures, Dusty decided that his strategy had worked. He did not allow himself to grow complacent. The fight was not yet over, nor was the safety of the battery assured. The Lancers had been hard hit by Company 'C's' opening volley and were continuing to lose men. For all that, they still had the advantage of numbers. If somebody could organize them and coordinate their efforts, they would still be a force to reckon with.

'Company "D"!' roared a voice, in an educated Northern accent. 'Company "D"! Rally around, men! Make for the guns.'

Attracted by the words, for they seemed to have sprung out of his own thoughts, Dusty sought for and located the speaker. It was the captain who had commanded the rear company; a tall, handsome, well-dressed and expensively equipped young man – but clearly one who knew his duty. He alone of the officers was trying to bring some kind of order out of the chaos. There was a chance, Dusty decided, that he might succeed if he was permitted to do so.

Although Dusty was interested by the captain's attempt to rally the Lancers, he did not permit it to hold all his attention. Which was just as well. He saw a burly, blue-clad soldier approaching to his right and was conscious of a second, on the left and to the rear, coming his way.

Hearing the shattering roar, and feeling the blast of the explosion, Colonel Middleton – commanding officer of the defending force – took his attention from the advancing Rebels. He stared for a moment at the smoking crater where the caisson had been. Then he turned his gaze to the three massive, cumbersome Volley Guns which had cost his small force so much effort and hard work during the forced march to Martin's Mill. Due to the accurate shelling, not one of them was able to operate. So, except as a morale factor, the loss of their ammunition would make little difference to the outcome of his mission.

Swinging his gaze to the Lancers, Middleton concluded that they would not be able to help him hold the Rebels away from the bridge. That was yet another point in his summation of the situation. Everything he could see told him that his position was rapidly becoming untenable.

From the beginning, Middleton had had little faith in his ability to carry out the duty in the manner which General Culver had demanded. It was, the tall, spare Infantry colonel realized, an almost classic case of too little arriving too late.

Colonel Middleton had been the first man to suspect where Ole Devil Hardin was intending to cross the Ouachita River and had suggested that an attempt be made to destroy the bridge. However, he had never expected to be given the assignment; especially with such restrictions upon his actions and so small a force at his disposal.

At a meeting of his commanding officers. Culver had agreed with Middleton as to the Rebels' destination and had given his orders. Middleton's regiment was to have the 'honour' of taking and holding the bridge, while the main force continued to 'drive' the enemy before them. According to Culver, all the 'Wisconsins' needed to do was stand fast and prevent the supply column from crossing. Backed by the half-battery of Vandenburgs and three companies of Lancers, they would – in the general's opinion – be more than a match for the Rebels' advance guard. Before any major assault could be launched, Culver had declared with his usual profanity, the rest of the Army of Arkansas would be on the scene.

Unfortunately, if not unexpectedly, things had not gone in the way General Culver had suggested. The task would have been more suitable to a cavalry regiment, supported by field artillery, but he had refused to use either. Nor would he give Middleton more men. Neither the Irish nor the Negro infantry regiments had been replaced, so Culver had claimed that he could not spare a larger force. Instead, Culver had dispatched the 'Wisconsins' with a small mounted screen of Lancers and three massive guns more appropriate to siege warfare than for rapid transportation. Apart from the difficulties of moving them, the Vandenburgs were basically a good choice for the work that had been expected. That they had failed was no fault of Colonel Middleton.

The limited time at Middleton's disposal had meant making a forced march and reaching his destination with exhausted men. They had been so tired that there had been no hope of establishing an extensive, strong defensive system, or of creating adequate protection for the Vandenburgs. On top of all the other problems, the Rebels' advance guard had come on to the scene far sooner than Culver – or even Middleton – had anticipated.

After that had happened, the whole affair had gone from bad to worse. First, although not unexpectedly, the mountain battery had moved in to counter the Vandenburgs. Then the company of Rebel cavalry had effectively prevented the Lancers from protecting the Volley Guns. Without the support of the Lancers and the half-battery, the 'Wisconsins' ' position was desperate. Certainly they could not hope to carry out Culver's original idea of retaining the bridge for his own Army's use.

There was only one thing left to do, Middleton decided. He must put his alternative plan into operation. It meant abandoning Culver's scheme and might even be regarded as a deliberate disobedience of orders. For all that, Middleton believed he was acting correctly. A humane, sensible man, he could not face the prospect of causing many of his soldiers to be killed in a hopeless fight. Far better, he considered, to withdraw across the river, destroy the bridge and keep as many men as possible to fight another day.

A lesser man might have called upon his second-in-command for an opinion, perhaps even demanded that it be put in writing and witnessed. Middleton refused to do such a thing. The decision was his and his alone. So he would make it and stand by the consequences.

'Go and tell the company commanders to prepare to retire,' the colonel said, trying to keep all emotion out of his voice.

'Yes, sir,' answered the adjutant, to whom the words had been addressed, adopting an equally neutral tone. Then he hurried away to deliver the message that might lead to Middleton being court martialled when General Culver heard of it.

Finding himself between two converging enemies, Dusty Fog's mind worked at lightning speed in search of a way out of the dangerous situation. A fast-taken glance warned him that he had no hope of avoiding both attackers. So he tried to work out a solution. Of the pair, the one on the left and to the rear was the nearer, and, therefore, the more immediate threat. So he was the obvious choice to be dealt with first.

There was, Dusty decided from his examination, one small point in his favour. Coming from that angle, the man had been compelled to pass the lance across his horse's head so that its pointed extended to the left instead of being directed straight forward.

With Dusty, to think was to act. Twisting slightly to the left, he lined and fired his Colt by instinctive alignment. As he had demonstrated to Billy Jack and the men from the Commissary General's Department in Arkadelphia, he was capable of considerable accuracy with that method of shooting. Flying true, the bullet entered the soldier's left breast and ripped into his heart. Shock and pain caused him to rock backwards and his left hand tugged involuntarily at his horse's reins. The animal responded to the signal and started to swing in the direction of the pull. In doing so, it ensured that the lance was turned away from the small Texan.

'Watch ahead, Mr. Fog!' Sandy McGraw yelled, who was able to see Dusty's peril but, being so positioned, was unable to help against the man in front of his officer.

The warning had not been needed. On firing, barely waiting to see the result, Dusty returned his attention to the approaching rider. He was not a moment too soon. Aimed to take him in the lower body, the lance's steel tip had already come by the head of his bay gelding.

Once again, Dusty's ambidextrous ability came to his rescue. Up flashed his empty right hand, cupping under and elevating the shaft away from him. The soldier yelled in fury, but was unable to prevent his weapon from missing its mark. Before he could do more than register a vocal protest, the two horses had swept by each other.

The Lancer was given no opportunity to recover. Coming up unnoticed, Sandy McGraw attacked him. Wishing to conserve the three bullets remaining in his Colt, the youngster dropped forward the top of his guidon. There was a spear-head mounted on the nine foot long pole, turning it into an effective weapon. The point took the man in his ribs, sinking until the quillons of the cross-guard – fitted to prevent the spear from penetrating so deep that the flag entered the wound – halted its forward progress. It was sufficient. Knocked from the saddle by the unexpected attack, the Lancer's weight dragged him free from the tip of the guidon.

Throwing a quick glance to where his first attacker's horse was swinging away, its rider sliding off of its back, Dusty swung his gaze to where the Yankee captain was still trying to rally men.

Even as Dusty started to ride towards the captain, meaning to silence him before he achieved his intentions, the matter was taken from out of his hands. Bleeding from a sabre cut on his face, a lieutenant rushed from the melee beyond the captain. Seeing Dusty approaching, the lieutenant – who had a scared expression on his face – tried to line his Colt. Just as the officer jerked at the trigger, the captain sent his mount in the small Texan's direction. He took the bullet intended for Dusty in the centre of the back.

Shock and agony distorted the captain's face. Clutching at the pommel of his saddle, he tried to hold himself on it. Failing, he fell beneath the hooves of his killer's horse. Realizing what he had done, the lieutenant threw aside his revolver. Before he could do anything more, Sergeant Weather appeared behind him. A swing of the sergeant's sabre almost tore the officer's head from his shoulders.

Although Dusty did not know it, the killing of the captain would be an indirect cause of much trouble and bloodshed in Rio Hondo County a few years after the end of the War.*

The fighting continued for a short while longer. Having emptied his revolver, without wasting a load, Dusty quit his horse's back. He acquired a discarded sabre and helped to engage some of the dismounted Lancers.

Then it was over.

Left practically leaderless by the disposal of their officers – being armed with revolvers, they had been the Texans' first targets – and having suffered heavy losses due to the unsuitability of their archaic weapons when opposed by firearms, the Lancers were demoralized and disheartened.

* How this happened is told in: *The Rio Hondo War.*

Some, on foot and mounted, threw down their lances and raised their hands. Others, who had stayed on their horses, turned to gallop towards the hamlet. The remainder scattered and fled in all directions. Eagerly a number of the Texans took up the pursuit.

'Bugler!' Dusty shouted, looking around him.

'Yo!' answered the musician, riding up.

'Sound "Recall"!' Dusty ordered, being determined to regain control of the enlisted men.

With the notes of the 'Recall' ringing in his ears, Dusty turned his attention to the main part of the battle. The howitzers were no longer barking and he realized that he had not heard the deeper note of the Vandenburgs. Already the leading wave of the Arkansas Rifles were swarming towards the first line of trenches, with the supporting Companies of the Texas Light Cavalry preparing to dash ahead.

An examination of the village told Dusty that the Vandenburgs had all been silenced before they could be brought into use. The assault had a better than fair chance of succeeding.

Which brought up another, vitally important, matter.

Swinging his gaze towards the bridge, Dusty heard the sound of shooting from the woodland on either side of it. From what he could make out, the detail sent by Company 'A' had run into heavy opposition and would not be able to reach their objective. Due to the denser nature of the terrain, he could see nothing of what was going on upstream. Perhaps Red and his men had also been halted. If so, the Yankees would be free to destroy the bridge.

Except that, by doing it, the commanding officer of the defending force would be trapping all his men on the northern side of the Ouachita.

Men were returning in answer to the bugle's repeated summons. Among them was Sandy McGraw, leading Dusty's bay, Billy Jack, Weather and Kiowa, the latter having arrived in time to take part in the later stages of the fighting.

'The sergeant major's cashed in, Mr. Fog,' Weather said.

'Damn the luck!' Dusty growled, but forced himself to remember his duties. 'Take six men and see to the wounded and prisoners, Sergeant Weather.'

'Yo!' Weather replied, turning and gathering the nearest six soldiers to help him carry out the order.

'Sergeant Billy Jack,' Dusty went on. 'Take rank as sergeant major. Form up the Company ready to move out.'

'Yo!' reponded the lanky non-com.

Having given the orders, Dusty looked at the hamlet. Encouraged by the destruction of the multi-barrelled weapons, the attackers were springing forward at a faster pace. They were within fifty yards of the forward trenches, with the cavalry galloping before them, playing a vital part in preventing the Yankees from concentrating their fire on the slower-moving, more vulnerable foot-soldiers.

Although Company 'C' should have been joining in the assault, Dusty decided that their absence would not have any adverse effect upon the outcome. They had already provided a most useful service by protecting the mountain battery. With their horses tired from the exertions of the charge and subsequent fighting, they would not be able to form up and reach the hamlet before the issue was resolved one way or the other.

At that moment, Dusty noticed something happening which aroused his curiosity and gave him cause for speculation.

After discharging a single volley, the occupants of the forward defences sprang from their trenches. They fell back rapidly, but – as far as Dusty could determine – under the control of their officers. Certainly they did not appear to be fleeing in panic. Passing the second and third lines of trenches, they continued to run towards the river.

'We've licked 'em, Mr. Fog!' Sandy McGraw enthused, sentiments which were echoed delightedly by the other men who were forming up before their officer.

'It's not over yet,' Dusty warned.

'If they go over the river, they'll be in our neck of the woods,' the bugler pointed out. 'We'll have 'em–.'

'Not if they blow up the bridge,' Dusty corrected. 'Then they'll have a better chance of getting away than they would from this side.'

'Don't we have help coming, Mr. Fog?' Billy Jack wanted to know.

'Gaylord's Dare-Devils and the Second Texas Infantry should be on their way,' Dusty answered, an idea starting to form as he looked at the hamlet. 'Colonel Barnett sent word to them to move up here as soon as our scouts reported about the Yankees holding the crossing.'

'Then we've got the bastards trapped,' the bugler insisted.

'Not if they can destroy the bridge,' Dusty warned. 'With that done, they can be long gone before Colonel Gaylord arrives from Arkadelphia. Reload those handguns, you men. Then we're moving out.'

'Yo!' Billy Jack answered, then eyed Dusty with interest. Unless he was mistaken, the young officer had something in mind. 'You-all fixing on us going to help run the Yankees across the Ouachita?'

'Nope,' Dusty replied. 'We're going to see how Cousin Red's detail are making out. When we've done that. I've got something else for you to do, sergeant major. But I'll tell you about it on the way.'

With the thirty men available to him, Dusty rode towards the woodland into which Red's detail had disappeared. He studied what was happening at the bridge and made sure that his earlier conclusions were on the right lines. Noticing that no defensive positions had been prepared on the southern side of the river, he felt certain that the Yankees had no intention of holding the bridge from there. So they must be relying upon destroying it to halt the supply column. Possibly they were under orders to only do so as a last alternative. Maybe General Culver had hoped to retain it intact for his Army's use after defeating the Confederate force which he was pursuing.

No matter what the original idea had been, the Yankees must now be committed to destroying the bridge. If they could be prevented from doing it, Dusty believed that there was a way to avert further bloodshed.

Quietly the small Texan outlined his idea to Billy Jack, whose gloomy assertion that it would not work – because of several highly unlikely accidents – showed that it stood a good chance of succeeding.

However, everything still hinged upon whether or not Red had been able to carry out his first independent and very responsible duty.

CHAPTER FIFTEEN

ALTHOUGH the soldier's appearance came as a complete surprise to Red Blaze, it did not cause him to be frozen into immobility. Letting out a yell, he jabbed his spurs into the brown gelding's flanks. As the spirited animal bounced onwards at an increased speed, he thrust out, cocked and fired his Colt. Fast-taken and aimed by the roughest possible instinctive alignment, the shot came *very* close to making a hit and partially achieved its purpose.

Hearing the bullet splitting the air as it passed close to his left ear, the soldier ducked involuntarily. In doing so, he caused the barrel of his rifle to lower at the instant when his right forefinger was tightening on the trigger. The Spencer bellowed, but its muzzle was no longer pointing at the redhead's chest.

A violent shudder ripped through the brown gelding as the heavy calibre bullet drove into its heart. Feeling the animal's legs buckling, Red kicked his feet free from the stirrups and tossed his right leg forward over the saddlehorn. He thrust himself clear of the falling horse, contriving to alight on his feet and running. While struggling to maintain his equilibrium and avoid plunging headlong down the slope, he swung his eyes towards his would-be killer. Being armed with a Spencer repeating rifle, the man was still a potential danger.

Horror was twisting at the Yankee's features as he realized his peril. Although the horse had been shot and was dying, its momentum was carrying it in his direction. Desperately he tried to fling himself aside, but he was too slow. The stricken animal crashed into him and he screamed in agony as its weight hurled him backwards. Horse and man went down the slope together. On top, the gelding was crushing the soldier between itself and the hard, unyielding ground.

After running almost uncontrollably for some yards, Red regained control of his movements and managed to stop. He hurried to where his horse was sprawled on top of the soldier. One glance told him that both were beyond all human aid. Looking around, he found nothing to suggest that the man had companions in the immediate vicinity.

Satisfied that he was not, for the moment at least, in danger of further attempts on his life, Red continued walking. On reaching the edge of the river, he went swiftly about making his preparations. For all that, despite being fully aware of the situation's extreme urgency, he refused to let himself become flustered or to act hastily. Instead, he thought out his movements with a care that would have surprised many of his elders if they had witnessed it.

If the main body of the picket had heard the commotion, some of them might come to investigate. Possibly he would be on his way before they arrived, but he wanted to try to avoid leaving obvious indications of his intentions. What he was planning to do would be sufficiently dangerous, without him needlessly adding to the risks.

Laying the Colt on the ground, the youngster divested himself of his tunic. He retained his dark grey shirt, but sat down to remove his boots and socks. Concealing the discarded items under a bush, he patted his breeches' pocket to ensure that Dusty's Russel Barlow knife was there. If he should succeed in reaching the bridge, he would need it.

With a final look around, to make certain that he had hidden the more obvious suggestions of what he was planning to do, Red waded into the river. His feet sank into the mud, but he thrust himself on until reaching deeper water. Taking a final look up the slope and satisfying himself that he was unobserved, he dived forward to start swimming downstream. At his point of entry, a gentle curve hid the bridge from his sight. Moving towards it, he kept constantly alert for any hint that he might have been seen by the enemy.

On reaching the bend, Red swam towards the southern bank. The current had carved a deep hole at that point and, even when close to the shore, his feet could not touch the bottom. Treading the water gently, with only his head above the surface, he let himself be swept slowly onwards and soon received his first view of the bridge.

From all appearances, the tide of the battle was swinging in the Confederate States' favour. While there was fighting taking place on the fringe of the hamlet, the Yankees appeared to be pulling back from the positions.

For a few seconds, Red was puzzled by the enemies' actions. They were retiring across the bridge. Yet they were doing it in an orderly manner and not in full flight. Then he started to understand their motives and realized that, now more than ever, he must do his utmost to prevent the destruction of the bridge.

Just as Red was about to thrust himself forward at a faster rate, he recollected his Cousin Dusty's often-repeated advice. The time to study the situation was *before* one became involved in it. With that in mind, Red allowed himself to be drifted closer by the push of the current and subjected his objective to a careful scrutiny.

The bridge had been built to handle plenty of heavy traffic and was of a sturdy construction. Unlike many of its day, it was not covered over as a means of protecting its timbers from the elements. Only a low guard rail was between Red and the soldiers who were already starting to run across. It would not be of any help in preventing them from seeing him. Fortunately, Dusty had taken that into consideration when planning how he would handle the assignment. He had told Red everything and the youngster was turning that information to his own use. So he knew how he could reach the bridge, but still keep out of the Yankees' sight.

Dusty had guessed that the destructive charge would be placed where it would do most damage. Bearing that in mind, Red looked at the massive oak central support and its Y-shaped bracing struts. Sure enough, a large keg of black powder had been placed in the angle formed by the southern supporting beam.

Sucking in a deep breath, Red allowed himself to sink beneath the suface. He did not dare go closer while on the top, in case he should be seen by the men who were crossing the bridge or upon the banks. Waiting until his feet touched the bottom, he started to swim just above the swaying weeds.

Soon Red's lungs felt as if they would burst. Grimly he forced himself to go on, for he had no means of estimating how close he might be to the bridge and had no desire to make a premature appearance. To do so under the circumstances would be asking for disaster.

At last, however, lack of air drove the youngster upwards. Above him, the surface was a circle of silvery light. Then the downstream portion of it started to become straight instead of curved. That would be the side of the bridge, cutting out the light. So he ought to be close enough to escape the Yankees' notice.

Something large, black and roughly oblong appeared, growing rapidly in size as it plunged downwards.

There was a crashing splash and Red felt the sudden turbulence of the disturbed water strike him. The mysterious shape came close and the younger's hands touching clothing. Silently cursing his lousy luck, he grabbed hold of the thing and confirmed his suspicions. Apparently a soldier had seen him approaching beneath the surface and had leapt over the guard rail to attack him.

Clutching his assailant by the front of the tunic and one arm, Red tried to prevent them from rising to the surface. He could not do it. Even as they started to ascend, he wondered why the man was not struggling to escape. He soon learned the answer.

Shaking the water from his eyes and filling his lungs with air, Red stared into the attacker's face. There was little above the eyebrows but torn flesh and splintered bones. The blood, tissue and brains had been washed away after being exposed to the water when a bullet had shattered its way through the skull.

With a strangled exclamation of disgust, the youngster released his hold. He watched the corpse drifting away, then looked upwards. Luck was still on his side, for they had surfaced under the bridge.

Another body plummeted over the guard rail, on the downstream side, almost landing on the one that had handed Red such a shock. Overhead, boots stamped on the planks as the withdrawl continued.

Swimming towards the upstream central support, Red had only the smallest worries regarding the way in which he would carry out his work. They did not come from wondering how he could reach the barrel. Company 'C' had visited Martin's Mill ten days earlier, before the start of the retreat, and Dusty had studied the bridge. He had formulated his plan from memories of that examination. The answer to how one could climb the support was simple – or would have been under less trying conditions.

Whoever had designed the bridge was clearly a man skilled in his work. He had included the means by which the bottom of the structure could be examined. Iron rungs had been driven into the massive central support, extending to water-level, allowing it to be climbed with comparative ease.

The only thing wrong with that, from Red's point of view, was the way the rungs were placed. On the *outside*. Which meant that, as he climbed up, he would be in plain sight of either bank; although there was sufficient of an overhang to provide concealment from the men who were crossing the bridge.

There was a shrill scream of agony and a third body tumbled into the river. Then a fourth followed. Bobbing up and down in the wash caused by their arrival and counteracting the thrust of the current, which was fairly strong beneath the bridge, Red took rapid stock of the situation.

A moment's thought told him that things might not be quite as bad as he had first imagined. Given just a smidgin of good old Texas luck, everybody would be too engrossed with their own affairs to notice him. Or the Yankees might figure he was one of them who had been hit by a Rebel's bullet, knocked from the bridge, but not so badly hurt that he was unable to try to climb back. Sodden by their long immersion, his shirt and breeches ought to look dark enough to aid such a deception.

Of course, one of the attackers might draw a similar conclusion and take the appropriate action.

'Yes, sir,' Red told himself. 'Things aren't quite so bad. Like getting thrown by a horse and being told you've only bust *both* legs, not your neck.'

Never one to worry unduly about the future, the youngster did not let the last thought depress him. Reaching for the nearest rung, he hauled himself upwards. Nobody took any notice of him as he ascended to the point where the supporting braces spread at angles of forty-five degrees from the central post. One shove would topple the keg into the water and the job would be done.

Or would it?

Placing his hand on the keg, Red started to notice things which caused him to revise his optimistic opinion.

Firstly, the keg had been carefully covered with waterproof tarpaulin.

Secondly, the Yankees had merely rested in in the angle and had not attempt to fasten or hold it in place.

Thirdly, despite having failed to take that basic precaution, they had gone to the trouble of arranging the barrel with the fuse on the *inside* of the bridge. Doing that must have been more difficult than merely sliding it in the other way round.

Lastly, as Red discovered when he climbed higher and seated himself on the unoccupied bracing strut, the fuse appeared to have been fixed in a haphazard manner. Not because it led to the southern bank. That had only to be expected. The explosion could not be touched off until the Yankees had crossed, so must be handled from that side What had caught Red's eye was the way in which the fuse had been passed loosely through the arches of the next support. Once it had burned beyond that point, its end would fall into the water and be extinguished.

Looking closer at the fuse, Red decided that it was unlike any type of slow- or quick-match he had ever seen. Taking hold of the fuse, he found that it was stiffer and felt different too.

It must, he concluded, be one of those new-fangled wire fuses that operated from something called an electric battery. Red had heard tell of such things, although he had had no personal experience with them. So he had an idea of the device's capabilities.

Somebody on the Yankees' side had been mighty smart and tricky!

The charge had been placed so that anybody who happened to find it, most likely being in one hell of a rush to save the bridge from destruction, would have reached an erroneous conclusion. Wanting to prevent the explosion, the rescuer would have shoved the barrel from its position and counted on the river to render it harmless. Instead, the waterproof covering would have kept the charge as lethal as ever.

Wriggling through the aperture, Red sat on the stout cross beam which permitted an examination to be carried out across the width of the under-surface. He tugged at the fuse, but it refused to return through the hole into which it had been inserted.

'I'm sure pleased this's Dusty's Barlow, not mine,' Red mused as he took out and opened the knife. Gathering a loop of the wire, he sawed through it. Letting the cut end fall, he sent the barrel after it. 'That's settled their—' he went on, but some instinct caused him to look over his shoulder. His relief ended and he twisted around, muttering, 'The sneaky bastards. They've put another barrel over there!'

Continuing to grip the open knife, Red began to scramble along the inspection beam. Over his head, heavy boots pounded incessantly as men poured over the bridge to what they hoped would be safety. From the various other sounds which had been, and still were, reaching the youngster's ears, the withdrawal was costing the Yankees dearly. Four more men had toppled over the guard rail, struck down by the Confederate bullets. If the screams and cries of pain that had repeatedly rang out meant anything, others had been hit and remained on the bridge, or were carried away by their companions.

Three harsh, sharp detonations from the southern bank caused Red a moment's anxiety. Then he realized that they must be shells going off. Having silenced the Vandenburg Volley Guns, Douglas Staunce's mountain battery had switched targets and were already bombarding the soldiers who had reached the other side of the Ouachita.

How much time did Red have?

Once the last of the Yankees had completed the crossing, the electric battery would be operated. The youngster had no way of knowing how the withdrawal was progressing. Of one thing he felt certain. If the remaining barrel of powder should be detonated, it would be powerful enough to wreck the bridge; or, at best, render it unsafe for the heavy wagons of the supply column.

'And it sure's hell won't do me a whole heap of good, comes to that,' Red admitted silently. 'If only the good die young, I likely don't have long to go.'

On reaching the second central support, the youngster once more tried to draw free the fuse. As with the other, the wire must have been knotted on the inside before the lid was fixed in position. However, Red did not waste time in idle conjecture over the reason for its immobility. The sound of shooting was drawing nearer on the northern bank. While the pace of the feet passing overhead was growing swifter, they seemed to be diminishing in numbers.

Either the wire was tougher than its predecessor, or the Barlow's blade had lost its edge.

'Come on, blast you!' Red gritted, feeling perspiration running from his forehead and down his cheeks. 'Cut through the son-of-a-bitching thing!'

Lead was flying in both direction across the river. Darting a glance to the southern shore, Red saw that the Yankees were forming up in whatever cover they could find and firing over the water. If any of them should see him, he would make an easy target.

Back and forward, back and forward, moved the knife without, apparently, making any impression on the wire fuse.

The last of the feet were coming closer!

So far, the Yankees' attention was directed at the soldiers of the Arkansas Rifles and Texas Light Cavalry. Swinging his gaze in the other direction, Red found that his comrades-in-arms were advancing through the hamlet, or taking up firing positions near the edge of the river.

Nearer came the last of the running feet!

Once they had crossed, whoever was handling the destruction would do what he had to do.

A savage jerk and the Barlow knife slipped through the severed ends of the fuse wire.

Giving a low sigh of relief, Red allowed the two ends and the knife to slip from his fingers. His work was not quite finished. While the barrel could no longer by ignited by electricity, a bullet into it from the southern shore would prove equally effective.

Just as Red was about to draw the keg inwards, yet another soldier's body was pitched from above. Instead of pulling, Red shoved and the barrel tilted from its perch. It landed in the water just after the man had arrived and, Red hoped, the extra splash would not be observed.

Before relaxing and considering how he might make good his escape, the youngster subjected the bottom of the bridge to a careful scrutiny. There were no more fuse wires, nor could he detect any suggestion that other barrels had been set out. So he decided that he had ended the danger of the bridge being destroyed.

And only just in time!

No more men were coming from the northern bank and the last of them had almost gone by his position. In a few seconds, the man responsible for setting off the charges would make his play.

Which raised the point of what Red should do next.

Should he remain where he was until the fighting ended, counting on nobody being able to draw a bead on him?

Or ought he to try to join his companions and tell them of the successful conclusion of his assignment?

Colonel Barnett would want to know for sure that the bridge would not be blown up.

The only trouble being that carrying the news to him could be mighty risky.

So, if it came to a point, would be staying put under the bridge. Once the expected explosion failed to materialize, the Yankees were sure to investigate. Even if Red still held the Russell-Barlow knife, it would be mighty inadequate. against men armed with rifles and several yards away.

A cry of agony shattered the air from above Red and the running thud of the final pair of feet changed into a fumbling stagger. There was a crash of something heavy striking the wooden guard rail and a blue-uniformed figure fell from the bridge. It was bare-headed, the face covered with blood, and wore the dress of a Yankee infantry's first lieutenant.

The officer was still alive. Plunging beneath the surface, he reappeared, flailing wildly in an attempt to keep his head above water.

'Help!' the wounded lieutenant screeched. 'Help me. I can't see!'

Nobody on the banks took any notice.

Watching the enemy officer being swept downstream, his struggles and calls for help growing weaker, Red knew that he would be drowned if somebody did not go to his assistance. Either the effects of the wound, or the blood flowing from it, had deprived the lieutenant of his sight. Whichever was the reason, he could not survive for much longer.

That was, Red concluded, a hell of a lousy way for a man to die.

Wriggling from the inspection beam, Red dropped into the water. Disregarding the danger of being shot by one side or the other, he struck out as fast as he could after the lieutenant. Red wondered how long it would be before a Yankee, or one of his own people, started throwing lead his way. It did not happen, so he concluded that both factions were too occupied in their fighting to interfere with the rescue.

Before Red reached the officer, he sank out of sight. Filling his lungs, the youngster followed. Finding the man, Red grabbed him under the armpits and, kicking out furiously, raised them both to the surface. On his head emerging, he immediately looked around. The current was thrusting him towards the southern bank. With the injured man hanging so heavily, Red doubted if he could hope to cross and reach his own side.

'Come on, feller!' yelled a voice with a Northern accent. 'Fetch him here. We'll help you!'

Swinging his gaze towards the speaker, Red saw a 'Wisconsins'[2] sergeant and a private running forward. More enlisted men used rifles to give them covering fire. They were on the fringe of the Yankees' line and would probably be part of the flank guard, Red decided.

Another glance across the river assured Red of how little hope he had of reaching his friends while towing his limp and unwieldy burden. So he continued to swim in the speaker's direction, drawing the lieutenant along with a hand cupped under his chin.

Seeing the soldiers continuing to wade forward, Red slowed his stroke and let them come until the water was lapping at their chests. The youngster was thinking fast and had seen a hope of avoiding being identified as an enemy. While his soaking shirt would be unlikely to give him away, the riding breeches were unmistakable evidence that he was not in the infantry. His bare feet might suggest that he was a Lancer who had taken to the water in a hurry to rescue the stricken officer.

So Red continued to swim even after he could have dropped his feet to the bottom. The soldiers reached out, taking hold of the officer and drawing him out of Red's grasp.

'Can you manage, friend?' the sergeant inquired.

'There's another wounded feller out there,' Red replied, trying to avoid sounding like a Texan. 'I'll see if I can help him!'

With that, the youngster turned and swam away.

'Hey!' yelped the private, staring after Red. 'He's wearing riding breeches and he sounded like a Reb. He ain't—'

'You're seeing things!' growled the sergeant, who had made a similar deduction. 'No Texan'd save one of our officers.'

'But—!' the soldier began.

'He saved Mr. Rint here,' interrupted the sergeant. 'So, unless you want to spend the rest of the War cleaning the officers' shit-houses, you'll reckon he's gone to save another wounded feller. Now let's get the hell away from here. The Rebs haven't shot at us yet, but I'd hate like hell to keep tempting them.'

Expecting to be shot at by friends or foes at any moment, Red struck out towards the northern bank of the Ouachita. He took a line that ought to carry him ashore below the fighting. The way he saw it, he had been shot at and taken enough chances for one day.

Directing a look upstream, Red grinned. The bridge was still standing, with only dead or badly wounded Yankees occupying it.

'They've likely tried to blow her up by now,' the youngster thought. 'I wonder what they'll do when they find that they can't?'

CHAPTER SIXTEEN

Riding alone from the woods fringing the Ouachita River, Dusty Fog was an anxious and worried young man. He wondered what his father and, more particularly, Colonel Barnett would think of the action he had just taken. It was an unusual one, but he felt that he had been justified in sending Company 'C' across the Ouachita River while he returned to make his report.

On reaching the woods with his men, Dusty had ordered them to dismount and continue on foot. That had been a sound move, for riders would have been impossible to control in such terrain. Moving forward, he had found that the Yankees' picket was already making a fighting withdrawal. The arrival of reinforcements had led to them all being killed or captured.

Dusty had learned of Red's departure from Corporal Hassle. So he had dispatched the old timer and Kiowa to see if they could discover what had happened to his cousin. With that taken care of, Dusty had pushed on to the edge of the woods. There, he had halted his men before they could be seen by the Yankes at the hamlet. To have continued the advance would have availed him nothing, except for needlessly killed or wounded men. Instead, he had watched the enemy crossing the bridge.

After the lieutenant who had ably commanded the rear guard was shot and had fallen into the water, the withdrawal had been accomplished. Dusty had waited with bated breath. The moment had come when the Yankees would try to destroy the bridge. Try as he might, Dusty had been unable to locate any trace of his cousin and wondered where Red might be.

When no explosion had happened, Dusty had been relieved and perturbed. Either the Yankees had failed to take the precaution of mining the bridge, or Red had been successful in nullifying their efforts. Yet there was no sign of the young lieutenant.

Kiowa and Hassle had returned with Red's property. From the story they had read in Red's tracks, Dusty knew that he had set off in the way that Dusty had outlined. That the bridge was still standing had suggested that Red had put the scheme to use and had pulled it off.

The question that had nagged at Dusty was, what had happened to his cousin after the conclusion of the mission.

While searching the banks in the hope of learning something about Red's fate, Dusty had given Billy Jack his orders. While the small Texan had known that he must place a whole lot of faith in his lanky temporary sergeant major, he had been satisfied that Billy Jack could be trusted with the work. Leaving his men to cross the river and carry out his scheme, Dusty had returned to the open ground with the intention of reporting to his superiors.

While Dusty believed that his father would approve of his actions, on discovering what had motivated them, he felt less certain of how Colonel Barnett would respond.

An infantryman to the core, Barnett had a reputation for being a stickler where military protocol was concerned. He was also said to have small respect for the abilities of volunteer officers. So he might be disinclined to accept suggestions from a very young and junior first lieutenant; especially one belonging to a volunteer *cavalry* regiment. Even more so when that same lieutenant had already implemented part of the proposals without having awaited their acceptance.

For all that, Dusty believed he had been justified and correct in sending the remnants of Company 'C' across the river and having given them specific orders on how they must act on the other side.

Locating his father was not difficult. Dusty saw Major Hondo Fog standing with Barnett and several infantry officers on the slope beyond the range of the rifles across the river. Guiding his horse towards them, the young Texan examined the battle-ground as they were doing. More than ever, he felt certain that he had acted correctly. He only wished that he could be as sure that Red was alive and well.

The Yankees had made good their withdrawal, Dusty observed, but it had cost them dearly. Yet the price had been lighter than if they had remained in the trenches without the support of the Vandenburg Volley Guns.

From the enemy, Dusty swung his gaze to the Confederate States' force. Making use of the Yankees' deserted trenches, or the buildings of the hamlet, the Arkansas Rifles were shooting across the river. The mountain battery's shells were falling accurately around the 'Wisconsins'' defensive positions. Already the three Companies of the Texas Light Cavalry were heading downstream. They would be going to swim over and either out-flank or take the Yankees from the rear.

Swinging from his saddle, Dusty handed the gelding's reins to the stocky Texas Light Cavalry sergeant who stood some distance from the officers and held two horses.

'You did good, Mr. Fog,' Sergeant Glissade praised. 'What happened to Cap'n von Hertz?'

'A sharpshooter made wolf-bait of him,' Dusty replied. 'Sergeant Major Goering's dead too.'

'It could've been worse,' Glissade commiserated. 'They was three to your one. Like I said, you did good.'

'*Gracias*,' Dusty said, knowing that he was receiving high praise.

'Your pappy was wondering why you didn't use the *caracole*, like Cap'n von Hertz aimed to,' Glissade went on, a note of warning in his voice. 'Maybe you'd best go and tell him.'

'I'll do that,' Dusty promised and turned away.

Walking forward, Dusty was conscious of the senior officers' scrutiny. His father – who looked like a taller, older, version of himself – showed relief and puzzlement, but the others displayed only the latter emotion. Schooling his face into what he hoped would be an expressionless mask, the small Texan came to a a halt and saluted.

'Lieutenant Fog, Company "C" reporting, sir,' Dusty said to the colonel.

'Where's Captain von Hertz, Mr. Fog?' Barnett demanded, returning the salute.

'He was killed by a sharpshooter while we were taking up our position in the woods, sir,' Dusty explained. "Our scout got the sharpshooter, but he was too late to save the captain.'

'That left you in command, Mr. Fog?' asked one of the infantry majors.

'Yes, sir,' Dusty agreed.

'You did damned well,' Barnett stated. 'Who carried out your assignment?'

'Mr. Blaze, sir,' Dusty answered and continued anxiously. 'Hasn't he reported yet?'

'Not yet,' Hondo admitted, watching the brief play of disturbed emotions on his son's face. Dusty and Red had been inseparable companions for most of their lives. 'I reckon he's safe enough, boy.'

'Where's your Company now, Mr. Fog?' Barnett wanted to know.

'I've sent them across the Ouachita, sir.'

'Under whose command?'

'My sergeant major's, sir.'

'Goering's a sound man, sir,' Hondo commented.

'He was killed in the attack on the Lancers, sir,' Dusty corrected. 'I appointed Sergeant Billy Jack to take his place.'

'He's good and reliable too, colonel,' Hondo declared.

'Why did you send them, Mr. Fog?' asked the major who had spoken earlier. 'And why didn't you go with them?'

'I felt it best that I should report to Colonel Barnett, sir,' Dusty replied. 'But I figured that he'd want a message sending to ask Colonel Gaylord to get to the bridge as quickly as possible.'

'You figured right,' Barnett declared. 'But not at the cost of sending a full Company to fetch him.'

'Only one man, Corporal Cotton will be going, sir,' Dusty

pointed out. 'The rest are waiting to carry out another duty.'

'You've told them to join up with the other Companies, huh Dusty?' Hondo suggested.

'Only if they can't do what I hope they'll be able to do, sir.'

'And what might *that* be?' Barnett growled.

'They'll try to convince the Yankees that our reinforcements are already on hand, sir,' Dusty drawled, retaining a flat, neutrally respectful timbre in his voice. This was the moment when he must lay himself open to recriminations, scorn, maybe even disciplinary action, if his idea should fail to meet with the colonel's approval. 'That might make them more willing to listen to your terms, sir.'

'*Terms?*' Barnett barked. 'Just what terms might they be, *mister*?'

'I wondered if we – you, that is, sir – could make them an offer—'

'Such as?' Hondo prompted, as his son's words died away and Barnett did not offer to comment.

'Giving them the opportunity to hand over the bridge?,' Dusty began.

'We've as good as got it now!' snorted the infantry major, but none of his companions appeared to share his sentiment.

'Yes, sir,' Dusty conceded tactfully. 'But I thought that we might be able to speed things up.'

'How?' Barnett challenged.

'We could offer them an exchange, sir,' Duty replied. 'Their freedom and an unrestricted passage through our lines for the bridge.'

'The Yankees wouldn't go for that!' growled the major. 'I know damned well I wouldn't!'

'I think the Yankee colonel will, sir,' Dusty contradicted, in the politest possible manner.

'What makes you think that, Mr. Fog?' Barnett asked, looking at the small Texan with added interest.

'The way he pulled back his men as soon as he saw the

Vandenburgs or Lancers couldn't help him, sir,' Dusty elaborated, decided that the question had been a point in his favour. 'Like you said last night, sir; the fact that the Yankees sent such a strong force, and not just a small detail to blow up the bridge, suggests they were supposed to try to hold it for their Army's use. Only I reckon their colonel was more concerned with the lives of his men and didn't aim to throw them away without good cause. I'm betting that, given a chance, he'll be willing to get them away safe. Especially if he believes that they're already close to being surrounded and cut off on the wrong side of the river.'

'The Yankees won't give in that easy,' insisted the major who had already protested. 'I wouldn't in their place.'

'Not even to save your command, what was left of it, from being killed or taken prisoner?' Hondo put in. 'Because that's what's facing the Yankees if they refuse our terms.'

'And if they accept,' the infantry major countered, 'they'll be free to fight against us again.'

'There'll be a lot of our men left alive who'd die trying to take the bridge,' Hondo pointed out. 'Because there's no easy way to do it. Time isn't on our side.'

'And if we give them enough of it, they could come up with a way to destroy the bridge,' another of the infantry officers remarked. 'Mr. Fog's idea could save us all that, if it comes off.'

'We'll give it a try,' Barnett declared, before any further discussion could take place. 'Will you deliver the terms, Major Fog?'

'I will, sir,' Hondo agreed, without hesitation.

'You realize that I can't allow considerations of your safety to influence my future actions if they don't honour your flag of truce and take you as a hostage?'

'I accept that, colonel,' Hondo agreed.

'Very well,' Barnett said. 'Is there anything you need?'

'The loan of a bugler,' Hondo suggested. 'And I'd like to take Mr. Fog with me, sir.'

'Mr. Fog?' Barnett repeated, looking from father to son and back.

'It's his plan, sir,' Hondo reminded the colonel. 'And the experience might come in useful for him in the future.'

'So it may,' Barnett conceded, nodding approvingly as his eyes returned to the small Texan. There was a very capable young man, with a great future. As such, he should be given every opportunity to participate in matters of importance. He looked the kind who would profit by doing so. 'I'll leave how you handle things in your hands, Major Fog. The rest of you gentlemen rejoin your Companies. I want everything ready to launch an assault, but I also don't want any mistakes if the call for a truce is accepted. We'd be getting ready to attack if we were expecting the arrival of reinforcements. So we'd best act as they'll expect us to. Don't you agree, Mr. Fog?'

'Yes, sir,' Dusty answered. 'I had something like that in mind.'

'Then why didn't you mention it?' Barnett inquired.

'I didn't reckon I'd need to, sir,' Dusty admitted.

'It's pleasing to find that at least one young lieutenant credits us old fogies with having a modicum of intelligence, Hondo,' Barnett commented dryly. 'Either that, or your son's a born diplomat. I'll not embarrass *any* of us by asking which you think it is. Go and attend to your duties, gentlemen.'

'I'll not ask if it *was* diplomacy, boy,' Hondo said with a grin, as they went to their horses. 'But I'd admire to know.'

'Colonel Barnett's one smart *hombre*, for a foot-shuffler,' Dusty obliged. 'I reckoned he might see reason, but he wouldn't want too much of it rammed down his throat by a wet-behind-the-ears, fly-slicer luff like me.'

'There's something in that,' Hondo smiled. Then noticing the way in which his son continually darted looks towards the river, continued, 'Don't worry, boy, young Red's all right. I'm willing to bet on it.'

'I hope so,' Dusty replied. 'If he's been killed—'

'It was after doing something that had to be done,' Hondo interrupted.

'But it was *my* duty to do it,' Dusty protested.

'You couldn't do it, through no fault of your own, boy. And Red couldn't have handled the Company as well as you did. You *know* that you made the right decision.'

'Even if Red was killed?'

'*Even* if Red was killed,' Hondo agreed. 'Because the destruction of the bridge would mean that a whole lot more than just Red would die. As it is, boy, once the Yankees accept your terms, we can cross the Ouachita and their main body won't be able to follow us.'

'Yes, sir,' Dusty drawled and, wanting to turn his thoughts from his cousin, went on, 'We'll need a white flag. I'll fetch one of those lances and I've a shirt in my saddle-pouch that'll do for it.'

'*Bueno,*' Hondo answered. 'Go to it.'

Mounting his gelding, Dusty returned to the scene of his Company's fight with the Lancers. Leaning over, he scooped up one of the discarded weapons without needing to halt or dismount. On rejoining his father and Glissade, he produced the shirt and fastened its sleeves to the shaft. At that moment, Sergeant Weather rode up.

'I've got your sabre here, sir,' the non-com announced, handing over the weapon.

'*Gracias,*' Dusty replied. 'Is everything all right with you?'

'Well enough, sir,' Weather confirmed.

'See to the men until I get back,' Dusty requested, sheathing the sabre.

An infantry bugler ran to meet the Texans as they rode down the slope. At Hondo's command, he blew the 'Cease Fire'. The message was relayed by shouted orders and the shooting ended on the northern bank of the river. After a few seconds, the Yankees also stopped using their weapons.

'Let's get going!' Hondo ordered. 'Show them the flag, Sergeant Glissade.'

'Yo!' answered the non-com, accepting the lance and elevating it so the improvised flap flapped in the breeze.

'Keep sounding calls, bugler,' Hondo went on.

With Glissade holding the lance upright and the bugler playing loud calls to emphasize that no surprise was intended, the party advanced. On reaching the end of the bridge, Hondo brought them to a halt. For a few seconds nothing happened. Then a tall, bearded Union infantry officer – whose shoulder straps bore the gilt laurel leaves of a major – strode forward and looked across the river.

'What's on your mind, major?' called the Yankee officer.

'A parlay, major,' Hondo replied. 'Will you meet us at the centre?'

'I will.'

'Can I suggest a truce for thirty minutes, while we're at it, to give us all time to attend to our wounded.'

'I accept that,' the Union major answered.

'This's as far as you and the bugler go, sergeant,' Hondo remarked, as he and Dusty dismounted.

Having handed their reins to Glissade, Dusty retrieved the lance from the sergeant and followed his father. The 'Wisconsins'' representative walked to meet them, followed by half a dozen soldiers who started to examine the dead and wounded men on the bridge.

'Major Fog, First Lieutenant Fog, Texas Light Cavalry', Hondo introduced, saluting. 'I'm here on behalf of Colonel Barnett, commanding the 1st Arkansas Rifle Regiment.'

'Major Grimsby, speaking for Colonel Middleton, 18th "Wisconsin" Heavy Infantry,' replied the Union officer and returned the compliment. 'May I ask what's on your mind, major?'

'Colonel Barnett sends his terms—,' Hondo began.

'We'll not surrender!' Grimsby stated grimly.

'We're not suggesting that you should. Instead, we're willing to let you come back across the river and offer you unrestricted passage through our lines for all your remaining men.'

'Suppose we say "No"?'

'Then a lot of men are going to die unnecessarily,' Hondo warned. 'You can't destroy the bridge. Nor can you hold it for long enough to let your main body arrive and stop us crossing.'

'That's a debatable point, major,' Grimsby countered, in a flat, non-committal voice. 'The Army of Arkansas—'

'Is still over eight miles away,' Hondo interrupted. 'And not moving fast. Long before it arrives, your regiment will have been wiped out.'

'You won't find *that* easy to do,' Grimsby warned, 'with the width of the river between us.'

'Our reinforcements on the south of the river have already been called on, major. Between us, we've got your regiment cold.'

'You're bluffing,' Grimbsy sniffed.

'Am I?' challenged Hondo, having kept the rim beyond the Yankees covertly under observation. 'Take a look behind you and see how much of a bluff it is.'

Turning, Grimbsy stared at the high ground about three quarters of a mile from his regiment's positions. A startled exclamation burst from his lips at what met his gaze. Lined on the rim were a number of Confederate cavalrymen. In their centre sat an officer, with what looked like a plume of some kind fixed to the turned-up left side of his Jeff Davis hat's brim. Such of the enlisted men who wore that kind of head-gear sported similar decorations. They were, Grimsby knew, the mark of members of Gaylord's Dare-Devils.

'Good going, Billy Jack!' Dusty breathed. 'You'll be disappointed, everything going so right.'

In accordance with his youthful commanding officer's instructions, Billy Jack had made the crossing and succeeded in remaining undetected by the enemy. After faking the plumes on the hats – with Sandy McGraw wearing Red's tunic and hat, having removed the ruined badge, to pose as an officer – the men of Company 'C' had moved to a position from which they could watch what happened at the bridge. Waiting until the parlay was under way, the sergeant had brought them into view.

Seeing the Yankee major staring his way, Sandy took off and waved his hat as if signalling to the Arkansas Rifles.

Then he turned and gave an order which sent Vern Hassle galloping away to the east as if going to report to the main body of the reinforcements.

'Like I said, major,' Hondo drawled, with the complacement air of a man who was holding all the winning cards. 'It's no bluff.'

'Maybe it's not,' answered Grimsby, trying to sound unimpressed. 'But it *could* be.'

'Calling it *will* cost you every man you've got,' Hondo warned. 'Those who aren't killed will be taken prisoner. Even if you'd prepared defences, we'd crush you in the end – And the end would come a whole heap too soon for you to carry out your original mission.'

Watching Grimsby, Dusty could tell that he was affected by Hondo's words and the apparent evidence of how close Gaylord's Dare-Devils were to his regiment. The major's eyes strayed to the dead and wounded on the bridge. Then he looked across the river at the hamlet. From there, he watched the last of the Texas Light Cavalry's supporting Companies as they disappeared into the woodland. They would come over and join with the new arrivals.

'I'll go and see what Colonel Middleton has to say,' Grimbsy promised. 'You'll have your answer in five minutes, Major Fog.'

'What do you reckon, boy?' Hondo inquired, as Grimsby marched stiff-backed in the direction from which he had come.

'He's convinced,' Dusty guessed. 'Question being whether he can convince his colonel. I reckon Middleton'll see reason. There's no sign of them holding Red prisoner, though.'

'He'd not likely be out in the open if they were,' Hondo pointed out. 'We'll ask Major Grimsby about him.'

The five minutes dragged by slowly, with Union soldiers carrying off the wounded and glowering at the two Texans. However, the truce was respected and nothing untoward happened. At last Major Grimsby returned and, although he was trying to hide his feelings, Dusty felt sure that the answer he brought was in the affirmative.

'Colonel Middleton accepts your terms, Major Fog,' Grimsby said quietly. 'If you gentlemen will accompany me, we'll arrange the details.'

Throwing another worried glance downstream, Dusty stiffened. A grin of pure delight and relief came to his face as he watched a horse bearing two riders appear from the trees. In front, guiding the animal, was a Texas Light Cavalry enlisted man. Behind him, without hat, tunic, socks, boots and weapons, sat Red Blaze.

The sight was all that Dusty needed to make his pleasure complete.

CHAPTER SEVENTEEN

THE crossing of the Ouachita River had been accomplished successfully by the Army of Arkansas and North Texas. Having preserved the bridge for their use, they had destroyed it as soon as their rear guard was safely on the southern bank.

On his arrival, General Jackson Baines Hardin had confirmed the terms accepted by Colonel Middleton. Not only had the remnants of the defending force been allowed unrestricted passage, Ole Devil had provided them with medical aid, facilities to bury their dead and transport to carry off the wounded.

Having dealt with that problem and the business of crossing the river, Ole Devil had organized his defences. There would be no further retreat, he had warned his tired but determined men.

Not until the next morning did Ole Devil receive reports from Colonel Barnett and Hondo Fog. Having done so, the tall, lean, hawk-faced general sent for Colonel Blaze and, after a discussion with the commanding officer of the Texas Light Cavalry, passed the word for Dusty Fog to report to him.

By the time the small Texan had arrived, his father had gone to carry out other duties. So Dusty found himself confronted by two of his uncles and Colonel Barnett. They were eying him with blank, hard expressions.

'Lieutenant Fog, reporting as ordered, sir,' Dusty said, halting and delivering a smart salute to the general.

'Let me compliment you on your handling of the Lancers, Mr. Fog,' Ole Devil replied, cold black eyes raking the young blond from head to foot. 'But I hear that you disregarded Captain von Hertz's instructions on how this should be done. He had intended that you should use a *caracole*.'

'Yes, sir,' Dusty admitted.

'You knew that?' Colonel Blaze inquired.

'I did, sir,' Dusty agreed.

'But you didn't do a *caracole*?' Blaze went on.

'No, sir. I didn't think that it would serve our needs.'

'Do you consider yourself a better judge of a tactical situation than Captain von Hertz?' Blaze demanded.

'No, sir,' Dusty replied. 'Probably the captain would have seen that, under the circumstances, a *caracole* wouldn't work. But he was killed before he could change his mind.'

'A *caracole* is sound tactics for men with firearms opposed by Lancers,' Ole Devil remarked, still studying Dusty with what might have been criticism. 'Why not this time?'

'The Lancers were in three ranks, sir,' Dusty explained. 'While we would have shot up the rear one, the other two wouldn't have been affected. They'd've been free to keep going at the battery.'

'So they would,' Ole Devil conceded and the colonels' faces broke into smiles which matched his own. 'You've done very well, Dustine.'

'Thank you, sir,' Dusty answered quietly, but could not conceal his pleasure at the praise.

'Company "C" needs a new commanding officer,' Blaze put in, looking at the general. 'I'd like to promote Mr. Fog to captain and give it to him.'

'I agree,' Ole Devil drawled.

'There is one point, general,' Barnett put in. 'While I accept that M— Captain Fog has carried himself in an exemplary manner throughout the affair, I feel we can't overlook the fact that he disobeyed his superior's orders. With the best of intentions, I'll admit, but to ignore it could establish a dangerous precedent.'

'That's true enough, Colonel Barnett,' Ole Devil conceded and the frosty expression returned to his face – yet with a twinkle in his eyes. 'You can't be let get away with it, young man. So I think that I know a suitable punishment. You'll need a new second-in-command.'

'Yes, sir,' Dusty said, wondering what was coming next.

'Colonel Blaze is promoting Mr. Blaze to first lieutenant,' the general continued. 'And he'll be confirming your appointment of Billy Jack to sergeant major. That, gentlemen, I feel is punishment enough.'

The smiles were back on the older men's faces, matching that creasing the small Texan's features. Dusty wondered what Red and Billy Jack would make of their promotion.

'All right,' Colonel Blaze ordered. 'Go and take over your Company. You're in command now, *Captain* Fog.'

Also by J. T. EDSON:

TO ARMS! TO ARMS IN DIXIE!

When Belle Boyd, the Rebel Spy, learned of a plot to organize the Southern States in an attempt to secede from the Union, she faced a problem. During the War Between the States, she had rendered loyal service to Dixie. At its end, she had taken the oath of allegiance to the Union and was now a trusted member of the U.S. Secret Service. Any clash of loyalties was averted when the Frenchman, a leader of the Brotherhood for Southron Freedom caused the deaths of two of Belle's friends. The Rebel Spy swore that she would avenge them . . . Even if she had to smash the Brotherhood to do it.

0 552 08971 0 25p

THE SOUTH WILL RISE AGAIN

While complete in itself, this is a continuation of Belle Boyd's relentless trail of vengeance on the Brotherhood, accompanied by Dusty Fog, the Ysabel Kid and Waco.

0 552 08972 9 25p
